MIRA GRANT

This special signed edition is limited
to 1500 numbered copies.

This is copy __1140__ .

IN THE
Shadow
OF
Spindrift House

In the Shadow of Spindrift House

Mira Grant

Subterranean Press 2019

First Edition

ISBN
978-1-59606-922-0

Subterranean Press
PO Box 190106
Burton, MI 48519

subterraneanpress.com

Manufactured in the United States of America

For my beloved Catherynne Valente.
May your lighthouse fires never falter;
may you always find your way home.

Part I:
Ebb Tide

Chapter 1:
The House of Angles

1.

Nature is a force of curves and spirals, of soft, radial lines feeding, one into the other, to form an interconnected web of compatible shapes. There are no straight lines in the organic world, only those which, through proximity to the softness around them, present the illusion of the ruler's edge. There is a curvature to the spine, the long bones of leg and thigh, the cutting surface of a tooth. Even the spider's web, vaunted architectural miracle of the insect kingdom, is curve upon curve upon curve when looked at with a discerning eye.

In all of nature, only three things may build toward true straightness, true defiance of the organic curl. Crystals seek a stark, lifeless geometry, line leading into line leading into hard, unforgiving angle. Viruses, which may be said to bridge the gap between the unliving, unthinking mineral and the hot, ceaseless tempo of the animal, form viciously sharpened cutting edges, turning their own mindless bodies into weapons.

And then there is the human race.

See how they build, planning their domiciles with care, measuring and cutting and planing until every line is straight, every angle is exact. They compete to build the straightest wall, the tallest spire, they cloak their organic curvature in line upon line upon line, and then they look upon the natural world—the natural world, which came before them, which birthed them, which will endure long after they are gone—and they judge it twisted and terrible, exclaim with disgust at the way it curves, the way it twists. They hate its softness, and hide their own behind wool and cotton, linen and canvas. They straighten their spines with braces and corsets, chase the curves from their limbs, conceal what cannot be made straighter, deny their origins, deny their eventual endings.

Humanity is an aberration, an affront upon all that is right and true and holy.

Is it any wonder, then, that the natural world, so hated, so denied, should look upon humanity with narrowed, furious eyes, should view humanity's rejection of the very forms which bore it as a betrayal never to be forgiven? And is it any wonder, with these things accepted and known, that that same natural world should look upon humanity and ask itself, in rage and in genuine wonder, if there might not be a way to cleanse this scourge from the broad back of the breathing, living, soft and curving world?

All time is limited. All time is passing. As humanity builds straight walls on bending, bowing cliffs and along the lines of rolling hills, that time passes even faster, offended until it flees into the future, where straight lines sag, where angles bend and break and fall apart, where the softness, freed from its geometrical bindings, can finally run free. This, then, is the punishment for those harsh lines, for those unforgiving angles: that humanity's time should run fast and hot and short, at least when compared to the other thinking peoples of the world, whose time is slow and cool and long, whose days are counted without number, and whose palaces, when they rise, rise in sweet, organic spirals, forgiving and forgiven by the eyes of the world.

Humanity has sacrificed so much on the altar of geometry, sacrificing eons untold to the mathematical aberration of the straight line, the perfect angle. Perhaps one day, they will see the error of their ways.

Perhaps one day, they will come home.

2.

We come, then, to the house, for the house must come first, before the people who will fill it. This is only right and just, for all things, straight and crooked, understand what it is to revere and respect their elders, and the house has stood for so long that it *is* an elder, at least to the hot-blooded, short-lived creatures who mill through its rooms, who exclaim with dismay over the state of the wallpaper, the slow, sagging settlement of the walls. We will walk its halls, if only for a moment;

we will peek into its rooms, and we will steal as much understanding as we can before the curtain rises and the show begins. This is the only opportunity we will have to see the empty theater, as it were; to see the bones of the thing.

Those who visit the half-ruined village of Port Mercy, Maine, are first greeted by the slope of the shore, which sweeps across the horizon like a glittering line, sand formed from the countless corpses of minute sea creatures. It is a graveyard for the small and a playground for the vast, as all graveyards must be, for tragedy is so often a matter of perspective. Most of the village has slipped into the sea, which reaches its greedy fingers a little further with every passing year, carrying the beachline with it, pushing sand deeper and deeper into the streets. One day, all of this will be gone, and the graveyard will rest as quietly as it ever has, only at a higher point on the land.

The few who still make their homes in Port Mercy are the children of those who have lived and died here for generations. They know that they will be the last, that their children, who laugh and play in the drowning streets, plucking seashells from porch steps and fishing in what used to be the school playground, will grow up far from here, never knowing what it is to serve the sea. Still they stay, mourning what was, mourning what even now is being lost. They will stay until they can stay no longer, and then they will be gone. Most of them have gone already, slipping away in the dead of night, where no one can see, or judge them for their failure.

Above it all, enshrined on a hillside so tall that the sea, hungry as it has become, will need to nibble and nibble for another hundred years before it rises far enough to tear it down, stands Spindrift House. The house is still straight and tall and proud, an architectural oddity rendered regal by the slow dissolve of all that lies below it. It looms, like some great beast of prey waiting for the perfect moment to strike and take that which was always meant to be its due. It lurks, a shadow in the reeds, a silent scream in the night.

It is not, in other words, a pleasing place to look upon, for all that its insistence on retaining its own straight, solid lines continues to draw the eye of those who wander too close, into the dreadful glare of its blank, unseeing eyes.

The story of Spindrift House is less than clear, although every local within a hundred miles—and most of the remaining locals are fifty miles away, in the sleepy, slowly dying lumber town of Norton, whose population has dwindled from its highwater mark of nearly two thousand to a far less robust three hundred and twelve—has what they swear is the true accounting of the cursed house and the people who once dwelt within it. For the most part, they agree that the house was built in the middle part of the 1800s, something which land grants and purchase records will support; the most likely date for the laying of the foundation would seem to be August 2nd, 1857. From there, the stories diverge, and quickly, becoming a tapestry of contradictions and oral traditions to impress and intimidate even the most stalwart of scholars.

Spindrift House was built by a rich fisherman as a gift to his dearly beloved bride, a French-Canadian girl who spoke little English, but who looked upon her rough-handed, rough-spoken husband as if he were a blessing from God Himself. When he failed to return home from a fishing voyage, she threw herself from the widow's walk, fearing that its name had been a prophecy, and broke herself upon the stones that ringed the house like silent sentries. Her ghost still walks the halls, weeping, waiting for the sea to show mercy and surrender the souls that it has stolen.

Spindrift House was built by a logger to fulfill a promise he had made to his father when he left the comforts of New York for the wilds of uncharted, uncultured Maine. It was meant to be a manse to put any in more ostensibly civilized lands to shame, but it was built without aid of a skilled architect, without the guiding hand of someone who could understand the vagaries of everything from wood to weather. At night, the halls creaked and moaned and grumbled under the weight of the wind, until the sound drove the logger mad, and he threw himself from the widow's walk in the very depths of the night.

Spindrift House was built for a widow who came to Port Mercy in the middle of the night with a fortune in her valise and a man by her side who she claimed was her butler and man of all trades, but who loomed easily a head taller than the very tallest villager. He never spoke, only stared at people until they learned to guess what he wanted, lest he look at them for even a single moment more. The house was constructed to her exact specifications, and she wandered through the halls at the end of every day, stepping around holes in the unfinished floor and over piles of construction equipment, making tiny, fiddly notes on the walls in white chalk, so that her fingers were always white as bone, and cold, so very cold. On the day the last shingle was laid, she pronounced the place perfect, paid her architects every cent that they were owed, and then threw herself from the widow's walk in full view of all the workers who had yet to leave the property. According to popular legend, she laughed the whole way down.

Only three things are agreed upon in all the versions of the story: that Spindrift House was built by someone who had come from away, not from the village itself; that whoever had built it, or ordered its construction, had died before the foundations could begin to settle; and that they had died by falling from the widow's walk.

This, then, is Spindrift House: built in the Victorian style which was then popular in most of New England, but which must have seemed strange and even hideous to the eyes of a small fishing village whose occupants had as little as possible to do with the outside world, home of modern temptations and even more modern corruption. It looms, four stories of artifice and artistry, with gables and filigreed porch covers warring for space with window nooks and the aforementioned widow's walk, which circles the whole of the roof, as if the sailors lost at sea might come from the tangled hillsides behind the house itself. It has belonged to multiple owners in the century and a half of its existence, and each of them has attempted to repaint the house, to make it over as their own. The sea air has faded most of those colors to a chalky, unforgiving brown, but when the wind is high, strips of old paint are sometimes torn aside to reveal rose gold, brick brown, and even a startlingly bright daffodil yellow.

Children from Port Mercy have made a game of seeking those strips of paint when they snarl in the bracken that covers the hillside, taking them home and carrying them as good luck talismans. They would never dare approach the house, but the paint is not taken from the house; it is taken from the wind and the hill, and those things purify it, cleanse it, make it safe.

If truly pressed, the braver among them might admit that the paint's allure is that it was given to Spindrift House and somehow, impossibly, managed to escape. Here, in the shadow of the sea, there is no more powerful act.

But come, come closer to the house, to the closed windows sealed tight against the damp sea air, to the shingles which cling, like barnacles, to the lines of the roof. It is a surprisingly sturdy thing, not moldering in the slightest; the curtains which block an outsider's view of the interior are frothy lace, unquestionably worth a fortune to some collector, who doubts or dismisses enough not to care if their new prizes come with ghosts tangled in their weave. No one has broken the windows. No one has scrawled obscenities on the walls or dug up the pipes for whatever treasures they might hold. Spindrift House has been allowed, for most of its long and lonely existence, to stand alone.

Spiders come and go through small cracks in the foundation, small gaps beneath the eaves, and here, in this liminal moment, between the story and the sigh, we may be as small as they are: we may follow them inside, into the hallways filled with cold, motionless air, into the rooms filled with antique furniture, covered in white sheets, like an invocation to the dead. The ghosts which walk here, through these elegant rooms, along these halls with their damasked wallpaper and their rose-strewn rugs, are nothing so simple as a sheet with holes for eyes and dust along its edges.

The ghosts which walk here are older and less forgiving than any childhood dream could dare to be.

Three stories of bedrooms and parlors and libraries, of washrooms and bathrooms with pipes that groan and grumble but carry water all the same, installed by an owner some fifty years back with an eye toward bringing the elegant old house into the modern era, of turning its eight bedrooms and many elegant sitting rooms into an exclusive boarding house for tourists seeking to experience the wild, unpredictable beauty of the Maine seaside. Three stories of shadows, of spiders weaving in the corners, of patches of sudden cold in the middle of hallways and in otherwise welcoming rooms. Spindrift House has had a great deal of time to decide what it wants to be, and what it wants to be is unforgiving.

The fourth story of the house is occupied almost entirely by attic—attic, and the small, plain room once intended for a live-in maid or nanny, tucked well away from the rest of the household. There is another, larger room behind the kitchen, intended as quarters for some more general house servant, but this room is tiny, tucked away, and easily isolated. It is more a prison than a palace, save for its view. This room boasts the highest window in the house, looking directly out across the seemingly endless sea. Anyone who sleeps in this room, dreams in this room, will be privy to all the stations of the tide, and will have the waves to sing them to sleep every night.

The door out to the fabled widow's walk is located in the attic. It opens easily, as if the hinges had been recently oiled; there is no resistance. The house seems to want people to circle its eaves, seems to yearn for the feel of feet on weather-treated wood. Those rare souls who have walked the widow's walk and walked away have reported difficulty getting the door to open again and let them back inside. It feels, to them, both in the moment and forever afterward, as if Spindrift House had been trying to offer them up to some great, inimical power, and had somehow been thwarted by their insistence on opening doors that would have been more kindly left closed.

There is no question that the house is haunted: that is simple fact, discussed as openly and frankly by the locals as the disappearance of Port Mercy, as the government's failure to admit that global warming and rising sea levels were condemning their way of life to one day become nothing more than a footnote in a history book that no one would read. The seas are rising, the weather is changing, and Spindrift House is haunted.

If only everyone were so willing to accept that which is both true and inconvenient, perhaps this story would never have happened. Or perhaps it would. It is a straight line, after all, from foundation to eaves, and nature abhors a straight line. Nature will do whatever it can to destroy both the art and the architect, for how else can things be made right?

These things are true: the widow's walk waits; the spiders sigh; and Spindrift House is calling its children home.

All the rest is details.

All the rest is coming.

Chapter 2:
In the Camera's Eye

1.

The difficulty with being a recognized member of a teen detective club is that "teen" was always a limited-time offer. No matter how hard we pushed the definition, it was inevitable that one day we were going to turn around and discover that we were, in fact, adults. Things that had been "cute" and "innovative" only a few months before were suddenly "reckless" and "immature." Maybe worst of all, we were suddenly expected to pay our own bills. And there were a *lot* of bills. Bills for things I had never even realized could cost money. For example…

"What do you mean, your dad isn't going to pay our insurance anymore?" I stared at Addison across the scarred wood of the kitchen table. "What do we need insurance *for?*"

"You know. Medical, dental, vehicle, personal injury—remember the Case of the Floating Mallards?"

"Yeah," I said warily. Floating ducks, not so unusual. Floating ducks who do it in midair, with no water anywhere in the area, without spreading their wings? A whole lot weirder.

"Old Mr. Jenkins got a broken collarbone when Kevin tackled him to get him away from that anti-gravity machine. He could have sued us. He *would* have sued us, if our insurance hadn't covered his injuries." Addison tossed her hair. It was perfect, as always, a silken waterfall of black, filled with flashes of blue and green and prismatic silver. I could live a thousand years and never understand how she hid so many colors in her hair. "Insurance is the 'get out of jail free' card that we all dream about having in our back pockets."

"Kevin was arrested anyway."

"Kevin maybe shouldn't have been buying his weed from a guy who sets up shop next to the 7-11 dumpster."

I laughed uneasily. That was another thing. When we'd *actually* been teen detectives, local law enforcement had been occasionally willing to turn a blind eye to our little transgressions—to Addison drinking with her boyfriend du jour behind the school, to Andy getting a little too physical when someone called one of us girls a name he would never repeat in our presence—as long as we were equally willing to let them take credit for our more marketable successes. Floating mallards or killer clowns, nah, that's cool, you kids keep doing what you do, but robbers? People who'd committed assault, or manslaughter, or in one notable case, serial arson? The police had always been happy to take those off of our hands.

The police were *still* happy to take those cases off our hands, but they weren't interested in offering us anything in exchange. Not anymore, not now that we could legally be tried as adults, not now that our guardians were no longer in a position to flip things around and go "oh, really, you want *them* to get in trouble when *you're* the ones who let a bunch of teenagers walk into a deserted gold mine with a serial killer, tell us how that's going to go again."

And yeah, maybe we gloated a few times because we were young and cocky and solving the crimes the police couldn't, and maybe we should have considered that something that was cute from a bunch of fifteen-year-olds wasn't going to be as endearing once we were out of high school. We should have realized that one day we'd be grown-ups, responsible for filing our own taxes and paying for our own insurance and, yeah, being a little more subtle about where we bought our weed. But that had always seemed impossible.

Ghosts? Sure. Robots and mummies and kids who thought it was funny to kill one of Kevin's chickens, draw weird glyphs with its blood, and try their best to raise the dead? Absolutely. Growing up? Nah. Never going to happen, not to us. Adulthood was the final mystery, and as long as we never opened our doors and announced our intention to unravel it, it would wait its turn.

Life didn't quite work out that way, of course. Life does what it wants, and damn the consequences. And here we all still were, stuck in a dead-end town whose only selling points were a remarkable tendency to attract the supernatural, the semi-supernatural, and the just plain weird. We were far enough outside Chicago to miss the exciting parts of life in the big city, and too close to it to be truly rural. Stuck in the middle, again and always.

"Look, Harls, the fact is, we're broke. We haven't had a paying case in months, Andy's the only one of us with an actual paying job, Daddy's done paying for our insurance—maybe it's time we admit this was a great hobby, but it's not such a great career."

I sat up straighter. "You don't mean that. You *can't* mean that."

"Harls…Harlowe. Come on." Addison spread her hands. "We all wanted to do different things, once upon a time. We were going to have careers."

"Yeah, only we found the mystery life, and you don't choose the mystery life. The mystery life chooses you."

"You're only saying that because—"

I put both my hands up, trying to cut her off before she could go any further. "Don't."

"—you're still hoping you'll figure everything out, and it'll all start making sense."

I glared at her. "We don't talk about that."

Addison had the grace to look abashed. "Sorry, Harlowe."

"No, you're not. If you were, you wouldn't go there every time you feel like you need to win an argument. But whatever." I stood. "We can talk to the boys tonight. Figure out what we want to do. Maybe you're right and it's time to hang things up, or maybe we can find a case that actually pays enough to keep us going for a little while."

"Or maybe we can split the difference," said Addison. "Find a case that pays enough to make up for all those summer jobs we never had, and set us up to start doing something else with our lives. Go out with a bang."

"Maybe," I said, and left the room. She was my best friend, the girl I'd been in love with for more than half my life, and I didn't want to look at her anymore. Not now.

Maybe not ever.

2.

In the beginning, I was the mystery and the detective at the same time, and that's the sort of thing that can give a precocious nine-year-old girl a headache that baffles doctors and makes teachers worry. No one thought I was faking: my distress at being unable to do ordinary kid things like "take math tests" and "read the encyclopedia" was too real, and okay, I was a nerd, which made my migraines even more believable—but no one really had the resources to deal with me, either. My teachers were preoccupied with trying to make sure my peers didn't jab each other with thumbtacks or eat too much paste. My grandparents were still, after five years, trying to adjust to being parents again when they thought that part of their lives had mercifully finished.

I was still waking up screaming every night, unable to explain my nightmares beyond vague impressions of knives and blood and my parents being dragged into a thick, oily fog, the kind of fog that sank ships and never returned what it stole. My shrinks all said that I was traumatized, and I guess they weren't far wrong. I'd been four when the police found me, strapped into my car seat and screaming my heart out, the butchered bodies of my parents still buckled into their seats, Mom behind the wheel, Dad reaching back toward me, so that his dead, cooling fingers had been only inches from my patent-leather-clad toes.

Yeah. I was a fun kid.

Maybe most third graders aren't obsessed with the mystery of how their parents died, and maybe most grandparents wouldn't allow that sort of obsession to take root and take over, but most grandparents aren't as broken as mine were. My father had been their only child, a sensible, sensitive accountant living in Hoboken, New Jersey, and they'd never expected the police to call with the news that he'd been butchered by some unknown cult, along with his pretty young marine biologist wife, and did they want custody of their four-year-old granddaughter, or should social services get involved?

They did their best to do right by me, and if their definition of "doing right" had included ignoring me for weeks at a time while I went over police reports and historical records and gave myself five-alarm migraines, well. They'd been grieving too, and grief is a monster. Grief is a beast made of teeth and claws and misery. I never needed anything else in my closet or under my bed: grief was more than terrifying enough. Some days I thought it was going to open its dreadful jaws and swallow me down whole...and some days I thought that might have been a good thing. After all, once I'd been devoured, I wouldn't have to wonder anymore. Why they'd been killed. What they'd done to attract that kind of attention.

Why I'd been spared.

Third grade had been almost halfway over when a weedy kid with limbs too long for his body and a black eye like the heart of a hurricane sat down next to me in the cafeteria, his own sack lunch dangling in his hand. I'd been having one of my good days. My headache was nothing more than a distant tingle in my temples, like the warning of a storm to come, and I'd been paging slowly through a history of cults in North America, aware that if an adult saw it, it would be taken away.

"Hey," he'd said, fixing me with his unbruised eye. "You're headache girl."

"Worst superpower ever," I'd replied warily. Kids didn't talk to me. At best, I was "that girl with the murdered parents," and was given a wide berth on the chance that being orphaned was somehow contagious. At worst, I was the nerd, the geek, the freak, the kid who actually asked for makeup homework and was allowed to go and nap in the principal's office when her head got too bad. Why that was viewed as some sort of special privilege, I didn't know. I would have been happy to trade my headaches for never being allowed to nap again.

"I-think-you-need-glasses," he blurted.

I blinked.

My father had worn glasses. They were one of the only things about his face that I still remembered clearly. He'd had my nose, sort of, and brown eyes, and glasses. They were in all the pictures my grandparents had of him, all the way back to when he was the same age I was now.

No one had ever, to the best of my recollection, tested my eyes. "You think so?" I asked.

"My big brother wears glasses, and he gets headaches when he doesn't have them, and sometimes you squint at the board, so I think maybe part of why your head hurts is because you can't see too good, and um, my friend Andy says you're really smart and I think there's a mummy in the old abandoned shopping mall and we're going to need someone really smart if we want to catch a mummy, so can you get glasses and then come over to my house?"

I blinked at him. He blinked back, completely earnest, and that was how I met Kevin.

IN THE Shadow OF Spindrift House

He'd been right about the glasses: I needed them, badly enough that when I actually *got* them, the entire world was suddenly called into question. How could I trust anything I remembered from the time *before* glasses when nothing looked the same *after* glasses? The world was suddenly possessed of edges and angles and straight lines, which were enthralling and repulsive at the same time, after so many years spent in comforting softness.

I'd showed up at Kevin's house the very next day, dropped off by a grandfather who was still going through the motions of raising his only grandchild, who had yet to start drinking in earnest. That was still two years in the future, coming fast and unseen, like an invisible train. Back then, I'd been nine, eyes huge behind the magnifying lenses of my new glasses, which didn't eliminate my headaches, but diminished them, whittled them down to something I thought I might actually be able to live with.

Kevin's house had been one more revelation in a world that was suddenly full of them. With my parents, I'd lived in a solid, sensible apartment, surrounded by other solid, sensible apartments, and I'd been too young to go anywhere on my own: my world had been limited to the things that could fit inside our walls, with occasional trips to the grocery store or the babysitter or the park down the street, the one with the gate that locked every day at seven o'clock, to keep out "the wrong elements." Whatever those were. And then I'd been with my grandparents, who lived in a small, somewhat worn-down house, the same one where they'd lived while they were raising my father. His boyhood room was still perfectly preserved. I slept in the guest room, making it over in my own image as much as I could, always terribly aware that I was somehow not a resident, but a visitor whose welcome could run out at any moment.

Kevin, though…his family lived in a little house set back not only from the road, but from the driveway, surrounded by a mass of garden beds and planters that rioted with herbs and beans and edible flowers. Chickens prowled the green, pecking at whatever caught their fancy, and a baby gate was stretched across the porch, keeping the dogs—there were six—from getting loose and running into the road, or devouring the chickens.

"We're a family farm, dear," said Kevin's mother kindly, when she saw the way I was staring. "Come inside. I made shortbread!"

I was an obedient kid. I didn't know how to refuse an adult, and besides, I'd come to see Kevin, not stand in the garden and goggle at the rampant growth around me. So I went inside, and everything changed forever, because Kevin wasn't the only one there. Addison and Andy were with him at the kitchen table, shortbread and lemonade in their hands, matching scowls on their matching faces, and I'd fallen in love in an instant, even before I'd had the chance to taste Kevin's mother's shortbread and realize that I would happily have sold my soul for the promise of more.

"Andy says you're smart," said Addison bluntly. "Are you?"

"Uhm," I said, because I didn't remember ever seeing either of them before.

Kevin came to my rescue. "Harlowe just got her glasses," he said. "She probably doesn't know who you are. Harlowe, this is Addison and Andrew Tanaka. Andy's in our class."

If I really tried, I could remember a dark-haired boy, as faceless as all the others once they were more than a few feet away, sitting by the window and never raising his hand. I nodded. "Hi," I said. Then, in a sentence, I sealed my fate. "I'm pretty smart."

"Good," said Addison. "We have a mummy to catch."

3.

Ten years isn't supposed to be the blinking of an eye, but I guess sometimes it is anyway, or at least that was how it felt to me. Hey! Presto! Your grandfather has a heart attack the year you start high school! Bam! Pow! Your grandmother tells you at the funeral that she's selling the house and going into assisted living, and hopes you'll understand! Whoops! Crash! Kevin's mother likes you enough to go through the process of becoming a foster parent in order to give you somewhere to go, and you wind up spending all of high school living with his family! College? No college: even the most predatory lenders don't want a kid with no prospects and no collateral, and I'd spent so much of high school focusing on mysteries that my grades weren't exactly awesome, which took scholarships off the table. Job prospects?

Well, that was where things got tricky. Because by the end of high school, we had nine years under our belts as mystery solvers and monster hunters and "those kids who were in the paper." Everyone knew our faces, if not our names. Everyone knew our roles. I was the brains. Addison and Andy shared being the beauty and being the bruiser, which used to make Addy livid, since people would inevitably try to imply that it was because she and Andy somehow mystically "knew Kung-Fu."

"There is nothing mystical about punching a jerk in the throat until he squeals like a rabbit," she'd say, and glare at anyone who looked like they might be thinking about arguing with her. "The whole idea is racist. This is a racist town. No wonder we get so many assholes pretending to be monsters."

I'd never quite followed that logic, but Addison had had that hair and those eyes and when she was angry she looked like she could do anything, and by the time I was fifteen I'd known that what I wanted her to do was me, as hard and fast and merciless as punching the aforementioned jerk in the throat, although maybe with less tracheal damage.

Kevin had politely side-stepped the whole question of dating by becoming totally obsessed with his pet chickens, to the point where his mother privately paid Addison a hundred dollars to take him to prom, just so there'd be pictures. I'd attended with Andy, naturally, and the four of us had posed under the balloon archway, his hand sweaty against my hip, and after the dance he'd gone off with Roy Malone from the football team and I'd gone off with Addison to sit by the creek and drink crappy wine straight out of the bottle and plan our futures while Kevin wandered around in the underbrush, looking for things he could poke with a stick.

"I'm going to miss this," she'd said, and waved a hand like she was trying to encompass the whole town, the whole world, us, them, everything.

"Miss what?"

"The mysteries." She'd been half-drunk, her cheeks bright and her eyes brighter, and she'd looked at me so solemnly. I would have done anything for her. "We were so good together. The four of us, we were so good together."

"Why do we have to stop?" I'd asked.

Maybe if I'd been brave enough to kiss her, she would have realized I was talking about us, together, and not the mysteries. Or maybe not. Either way, I wasn't brave enough, and I didn't kiss her, and she'd pulled back and looked at me thoughtfully, and then she'd smiled, and the future had been chosen.

Nine years of mysteries and masks and monsters before graduation and one year after, and we did a lot of good, we really did. We solved a lot of crimes, some explicable, some inexplicable, and if we never caught a real monster, we still knew they existed. We just needed to pin one of them down, and everything would change.

And the whole time, I'd been digging into the deaths of my parents, just like I did when I was nine years old, giving myself headaches as I squinted at crime scene photos I probably shouldn't have been allowed to see, reading police reports, and hoping, and hoping, and hoping. Hoping that today would be the day when all of this started making sense.

I had found a few leads, over the years. A few directions we could point ourselves in, a few people we could question. Some of them, I'd shared with the group. Others, I'd kept close to my chest. I went to my room and closed the door, checking twice to be sure the latch had caught. Then I reached for my bag and pulled out my scrapbook, opening it as I sat down on the bed.

Addison wanted a big score. I wanted to keep the band together—and if that wasn't possible, I still wanted them beside me while I made one last attempt to find out what had happened to my parents. I knew, deep down, that if I was ever going to get my answers, I was going to get them in the company of the only people who had known and loved me since grade school, the people who looked at me and saw Harlowe Upton-Jones, cryptography fanatic, mystery freak, beloved nerd. The rest of the world seemed to read the lines of tragedy written in my face, but these, my friends, my virtual family…they were the only people who could potentially get me home.

I tapped the headline on the last page of the book, the article I'd been keeping to myself for the better part of a year. Addison wanted a payday and I wanted to remind her why this was what we did with our lives.

Spindrift House was going to make sure we both got what we wanted.

4.

The kitchen table—I still thought of it as "Kevin's kitchen table," even after all this time, even after five years of calling his house my home—was a little older and more battered than it had been the first time I sat down at it, but the four of us still fit around it, in the same order we always had. Addison and Andy, side by side, close enough that they could bump shoulders when they needed to comfort themselves with the evidence that they weren't alone; Kevin on Andy's other side, further away, giving himself the space he so direly needed. The last of the most recent pack of dogs sat next to him, geriatric head resting on Kevin's knee as she peered upward with bleary, adoring eyes. She was probably going to be the last dog for a while. Kevin loved his chickens more than he loved anything else, and the dogs had a tendency to chase and bother them.

Not Petunia. She was sixteen in human years and ancient in dog years, and she had seen every other one of the dogs who'd met me at the door on my first visit consigned to the small pet cemetery at the back of the property. She didn't want to chase chickens or bother cats or do anything other than love Kevin with every ounce of strength in her failing canine frame. And fart. Before moving in with Kevin's family, I had never realized how much a dog could *fart*.

"I have a case," I said.

Kevin stopped talking to the dog. Addison stopped scrolling through her Twitter mentions. Andy, who had already been listening to hear what I was going to say, didn't do anything. Andy liked our meetings better than anyone else. He liked having a clear idea of what we were going to do.

"Paying?" asked Addison.

"Yes and no," I said.

She raised one perfectly shaped eyebrow and waited.

When we had to be on camera—which was more frequent than not—Addison was our go-girl. She was smart, she was a fast talker, and she was willing to do the work to elevate herself from "pretty" to "ready for my closeup." She viewed femininity as one more weapon she could slot into her not inconsiderable arsenal, and as long as she was doing it, I didn't have to.

"Have any of you heard of Spindrift House, out in Maine?"

Silence greeted this question, stretching out long enough that I was about to resume my planned speech when Andy, slowly, nodded.

"Haunted, right?" It could have been a guess. Coming from Addison, it *would* have been a guess: she liked to sound like she knew what was going on, and was a master of leaving pauses that people would fill in for her, allowing her to maintain the illusion of omniscience. Andy, though. Andy didn't guess, and he didn't dissemble. Andy waited until he *knew.* "There was something about it in last year's Paranormal Society roundup."

"It's one of the last great reward locations," I said, and handed Kevin my stack of folders. As he passed them around the table, I continued, "There are three families who claim ownership, which wouldn't matter much, if the house didn't come with approximately two thousand acres of land above the projected high-water mark for the next decade."

Kevin frowned. "Two hundred acres is nice, but—"

"Not two hundred: two *thousand.* Will it still be there in thirty years? Maybe not. But right now, it's fertile, it's salable, and it's attached to the land deed for the house. Whoever owns Spindrift owns basically all the land above the nearest town, a fishing village called 'Port Mercy.'" All of this was in the folders, but everyone learns differently. An impassioned verbal delivery can go a long, long way toward getting people on my side. "Of the three families who claim ownership, two are more than reasonably wealthy, and would like to be wealthier. So they've been offering a reward."

"How big?" asked Addison, flipping through her folder. Then she paused, eyes widening as they snagged on the number. "Oh. *Oh.* And this is legit?"

"It is. Three point five million dollars to the person or people who can go into the house and stay there long enough to find the original deed."

Andy's frown was even deeper than Kevin's had been. "There has to be some sort of a catch."

"There are several," I said. "For one thing, remember that there are *three* families involved, and only two of them are offering the reward. They had to get the third family to agree to it, and that means the third family actually had some bargaining power. First catch, we have to agree to a full search of our persons and possessions before we'll be allowed to enter the house, to make sure we're not trying to smuggle in a falsified land deed that would award the property to a specific family. That's one of the terms all three families are okay with, since I'm pretty sure by this point, they're all willing to cheat."

Andy, who didn't like anyone seeing him naked, looked faintly ill. "First catch. What's the second?"

"Second catch, once we enter the house, we're not allowed to leave it," I said. At their alarmed expressions,

I clarified, "We can go outside—they'll have a guard posted the whole time, and they don't want us to get cabin fever in there—but only as far as the original fence line. No one comes in, no one goes out. If we want to have food delivered, it gets checked by the guard before it comes to us, and we don't get anything with writing on it. Not even receipts. Although I'm told that, for tax purposes, those will be kept for us until we give up."

"The way you say that makes me think there's a third catch," said Addison.

"There is." I took a deep breath. This was either the major selling point or the nail in my coffin, depending on how everyone else was feeling. Andy loved our more "monster-centric" work. Addison saw it as frivolous, the reason we couldn't get anyone to take us seriously. Kevin fell somewhere in the middle, and could go either way.

"The house is haunted," I said.

Addison was unmoved. "Lots of houses are haunted."

"The house is haunted to the extent that several people who've signed up to solve this exact mystery have been found dead by the guards, who are instructed to enter if they don't see any of us for twenty-four hours,"

I said. "None of the bodies have shown any obvious cause of death, leading people to conclude—"

"If you say that they were scared to death, I will punch you in the throat," said Addison pleasantly.

I closed my mouth with an audible click.

Again, she raised one perfect eyebrow. "Really? That's the story they're going with?"

"It's a lot of money," I said.

"It is, which makes me wonder why you waited so long to bring it to us." She tilted her head. "What aren't you saying?"

"The three families who claim ownership of the land are the Latours, the Pickwells, and the Uptons." I took a deep breath. "My mother's family. They're the ones without any money. They're the ones who insisted that the doors be locked behind anyone who wanted to go inside. I found out about the house because I was trying to find my parents."

"Ah." Addison looked at me thoughtfully for a moment. Then, without any further ado, she nodded and rose. "Get your stuff, everybody. We're insured through the end of the month, and it looks like we're going to Maine."

Chapter 3:

Homecoming

1.

We all knew our roles, once we were on the road and heading toward our latest mystery. It was familiar, even comforting, because these were the simplest, most predictable versions of ourselves. Once we reached Spindrift House, nothing would be simple, or predictable. We were counting on it. The word for a simple, predictable mystery is "solved."

Andy and Addison always took turns driving. My eyesight was too bad, and Kevin's anxiety made him prone to swerving whenever he saw anything in the road, insisting that the rock had been a turtle, the branch had been a snake, and the flapping plastic bag had been the Mothman. So Andy and Addy split the front while Kevin and I sat in the back of the Subaru station wagon that had originally belonged to his mother, me squinting at the screen of my laptop and him flipping through sheaf after sheaf of printed paperwork.

"There's no internet at the house," he said, for the eighth time.

"That's why we have printouts." The instructions from the families overseeing the reward had indicated that bringing *some* paper in was just fine, as long as we didn't mind it being tested to within an inch of its fibrous existence. No counterfeit land deeds, no fake wills. Blueprints and eyewitness accounts of the haunting? Sure, whatever.

"Can we stop at the border? There's a weed store there that has really good reviews."

"Sure, Kevin." I raised my voice. "Addy, you hear that?"

"Pot store," she said. "Got it."

Kevin looked relieved, and went back to thumbing through the paperwork that would become our only protection against whatever wonderful terrors awaited.

All four of us had our reasons for staying in town and staying together. In Addison's case, it was Andy's calm refusal to look at colleges outside of driving distance. Andy understood our hometown. He knew the rules there, and how to follow them. He liked it when things followed the rules. He liked knowing up was up, down was down, spare toilet paper was in the linen closet, and fresh meat went on the shelf at the grocery store every morning at six-fifteen a.m. sharp. Addison had always hoped to go someplace far-off and new, like UC Santa Cruz or Washington State, but she wasn't willing to go anywhere that didn't include her brother. He kept her on an even keel. He always had.

Me, I didn't have the money to pay for college and I didn't have the grades or extracurriculars to get a scholarship, and while "I'm pretty sure my parents were killed by weird cultists and I don't know why I was spared" might make a hell of a personal essay, it seemed unlikely to unlock any of the greater institutions of learning, unless I wanted to go to Miskatonic.

They would probably have seen "cultists killed my parents" as a bonus.

I did not want to go to Miskatonic. I wanted to attend a school where the number of surviving graduates exceeded the number on the "In Memoriam" page of the yearbook. And even if I'd wanted to go, the lack of financing would still have kept me standing on the sidewalk, looking in and wishing things were different.

As for Kevin…Kevin had anxiety. Maybe that's a strange thing in a professional mystery-chaser, ghost-hunter, and monster-facer, but the things we did were *normal* for him. They were ordinary, everyday things, things he shared with his friends and his makeshift almost-sister. They were things that left him with the time to spend coddling his chickens and getting royally baked, and we didn't judge. We'd been there when it started, we knew how bad it could get, and we loved him anyway. He was our Kevin. One of the kindest, most generous men in the entire world. College would never have been as kind or as understanding as we were, and he'd known that he wanted to stay with us for as long as possible, and so there had been no point, for him, in even applying for anything away from home.

His mother had been understanding. His father had been long out of the picture. Kevin and I had stayed at home, and helped with the farming and the chores, and the fact that we didn't want to go had become, bit by bit, something like a blessing. Addison and Andy's parents had been less enthusiastic, but Addison had never in her life met a problem she couldn't convince to become an opportunity, and she'd managed to talk them around, right up until her father decided he didn't want to pay for our insurance anymore.

This was our last chance to show that we could make it as a group, and maybe also my last chance to find out something—anything—about what had happened to my parents. Nothing about them should have been important or dangerous enough to have attracted the attention of a cult. I'd spent my life waffling back and forth on whether they'd been in the wrong place at the wrong time, or whether my grandparents had never known their son as well as they wanted to pretend that they had. "Wrong place, wrong time" was tempting for the absolution it offered, but didn't explain why I'd been spared. My grandparents not knowing as much as they thought they did...

53

Well. I had grown less charitable toward them over the years. Maybe there was something to the idea that they'd been left pleasantly in the dark, rather than asking them to accept that their precious boy had somehow gotten involved with something they wouldn't have approved of.

The drive from Chicago to Port Mercy was supposed to take a little over seventeen hours, assuming we didn't stop at all. There was no way that was ever going to happen. We needed to eat, we needed to gas up, we needed to change drivers, and we needed to give Kevin smoke breaks, since he was saving his edibles for the house. We were all long since accustomed to the faint, lingering aroma of skunk that clung to his hands and clothes—I even found it comforting, sometimes, a reminder of the foster brother who would break the world for me—but that didn't mean we wanted to be hotboxed.

By the end of the first day, we had gone slightly more than a third of the distance, and we piled into our hastily-selected motel rooms with the fervor of pilgrims on the road to an untried and somewhat questionable destination. As usual, we paired off brother-sister, since Andy wasn't comfortable sleeping around anyone but Addison, and we really couldn't afford three rooms.

There were some rumors, back in high school, about me and Kevin, and I guess I can understand that, even as the very thought made Kevin recoil in horror while I laughed myself to the point of nausea. If he hadn't been born my brother, he had still *become* my brother the day his mother told the state of Illinois that she'd be happy to take care of me, and given how little my blood family had done to keep me safe and healthy, I wasn't going to do anything—*anything*— to endanger the family that had chosen me when I had nothing.

Besides, Addison snored, and if I could avoid that, I considered myself to be doing pretty well.

That first night, I slept peacefully, only to wake up and find Kevin sitting on his bed, watching me, a concerned frown on his face.

"What?" I asked, lisping slightly around my mouth guard.

"You were crying," he said. "In the middle of the night. I got up to use the bathroom, and you were crying. Are you okay, Harley? Is everything all right?"

"I must have had a bad dream." I touched my cheek. My fingers came away dry. "Whatever it was, I clearly got over it, and I don't remember anything.

Let's go. I want to convince Addison that we can go to a diner, instead of another McDonald's drive-through."

Kevin had to take a smoke break twice as long as his normal ones before he felt up to getting in the car. We all chalked it up to nerves. This wasn't the longest road trip we'd ever taken in the pursuit of a case, but it was certainly the one where the stakes were highest. Win this prize and stay together. Fail, and…

We'd figure something out. We always figured something out, when we absolutely had to.

Our first day's success had clearly gone to Addison's head, because not only did she veto the diner, she vetoed the drive-through until we were thirty miles out of town, an arbitrary number that became a countdown that became a narrowly avoided speeding ticket. Andy took over driving for a while after that, while Kevin dozed in the backseat and I tried to pretend that I didn't feel the miles wrapping around me in a sort of enveloping sensation of dread. I wanted to turn around. We couldn't turn around. I couldn't even explain why I thought we *should*.

This had all been my idea. I was the one whose relatives, however distant, however unaware of my existence, wanted to prove their ownership of Spindrift

House. I was the one who didn't want to let go of the one thing I had ever been both good at and happy doing with my life. So why was I also the one throwing up in gas station bathrooms, facing myself in the mirror and unable to quite recognize the girl reflected there?

I've never been what the poets would call a "great beauty." I somehow managed to inherit the worst aspects of both my parents: my father's fine, lank hair, which seems to view any change of the weather as an excuse to become frizzy and tangled and impossible to tame, and my mother's slightly sallow complexion, which looked amazing in all the pictures I could find of her, paired as it was with her sleek black hair and wide gray eyes. Well, I got her eyes, but I also got my father's lousy eyesight. Glasses plus eyes a little too big for the rest of my face meant that I always looked like I was wearing swim goggles, making me seem alien and a little off-putting. Even if I hadn't been hopelessly in love with Addison basically from the word "go," I would never have been at the top of anyone's list of social butterflies.

Now, though…the road trip seemed to be stealing what little color I possessed from my cheeks, leaving me as pale and unsettlingly greenish as a waterlogged corpse. I wasn't keeping much of anything down, and my cheeks were hollow, beaten for gauntness only by the sunken black circles around my eyes. I glared at me, oddly relieved when my reflection glared back.

"Nerves," I said. "This is all just nerves, and you'll be fine when we get to Maine."

The toilet flushed in one of the stalls behind me. The door opened, and Addison emerged. "Talking to yourself now?" she asked. "That's a bold choice."

"Yeah, well, sometimes I need a bit of decent conversation." I splashed water on my face, trying to make it less obvious that I looked like hell.

It didn't work. "You look like hell," said Addison bluntly, stepping up to the sink next to mine and starting to wash her hands. "Did you sleep last night?"

"Not really."

"You should sleep tonight." This time the look she gave me was concerned. "Ask Kevin if he can spare one of his magic cookies or something."

"I don't need to be stoned to sleep," I protested.

"Need, no, but would it *help?*" Addison turned away from the sink. "We'll be in Port Mercy tomorrow. Things will go more smoothly if you've rested."

"I'll try," I said.

She reached over and squeezed my shoulder. "That's what matters here, okay? We all just need to try. I'll see you at the car."

I watched her reflection in the mirror as she walked to the door. She had a wiggle in her hips and her usual, almost arrogant angle to her head, and I loved her in that moment as I had loved her almost all my life, and I almost shouted for her to stop, almost told her that we were making a mistake. I swallowed the words before they made it past my lips. We were here because of me. I would swipe one of Kevin's cookies. I would sleep fine. We would make it to Spindrift House, and everything would be *fine*.

It had to be.

2.

Despite the pot in my system, I woke up screaming shortly after midnight, clawing at the air like I thought I had been buried alive, like I thought I could push the oppressive weight of the onrushing future away and allow myself to breathe. Kevin was sitting on my bed less than a second later, folding his arms around me, solid, comforting, and absolutely real in the same way he had always been, the same way I knew he'd always be. I buried my face against his shoulder, shaking hard, and let him hold me.

Kevin didn't say a word. He knew me better than any of the others, brother in all but blood, and he knew that while his anxiety might be harder to dismiss, mine—on the rare occasions where it raised its ugly head—was just as bad. Orphaned, unwanted, unable to let go, I had a laundry list of excellent reasons to be unhappy, and only the fact that Kevin and his family had been there to catch me when my grandparents finally gave up on holding the rope had been enough to prevent me from toppling into the abyss.

Eventually, my tears stopped and I pulled my face from his shoulder, resting my cheek against the smooth slope of his upper arm. He smelled of motel soap and marijuana, and both of those things were comforting, whether or not they should have been.

Kevin kissed the top of my head. "You want to talk about it?" he asked.

"No," I said. I wasn't sure I *could* talk about it. The last cobwebby strands of my dreams were dissolving into a mush of ill-feeling and faint, psychosomatic nausea. All they were leaving behind was the faint impression of the thick, oily fog that I had always dreamt devouring my parents, and the crashing of some unseen, unseeable sea.

"Okay." Kevin squeezed me a little tighter. "You want to go outside and get ripped next to the pool?"

I thought about it. Then I nodded.

"Yeah," I said. "That sounds good."

We smoked two blunts, laughing and dangling our feet in the water. The motel security guard came around, intending to chase us away, and was easily bribed with a few hits off Kevin's expertly-rolled joint into pretending he hadn't seen a thing. We returned to bed just before dawn, and woke at eight to the sound of Addison pounding on our door and shouting for us to get our butts in the car already, we still had a full day's drive ahead of us. Kevin looked at me and giggled, groggy in his boxers, face unshaven and still as sweet and familiar as it had been on the day we met.

I giggled back, and thought that maybe the worst was behind us. My nerves would stop trying to eat me alive; we would get to Spindrift House, solve the mystery, cash the check, and never have to worry about money again. We'd be able to stay together.

Soon enough, this would all be over.

How right—and how wrong—I was.

3.

The representatives of the Latour and Pickwell families were waiting for us next to the faded, dry-rot-riddled sign welcoming visitors to Port Mercy, Maine, which was—apparently—"A Healthy Place for Families."

The fishing village that spread out at the base of the low rise where the road ran and the sign was mounted didn't look like it was in the business of being healthy for anyone, much less for families. Half the houses had collapsed in on themselves, their foundations undermined by the slow, inexorable spreading of the sea. The houses that still stood looked, for the most part, like they wouldn't be standing much longer, even as they bore the distinct marks of habitation: cars in the driveways, lights in the windows.

It was like watching the last patches of healthy flesh fighting not to succumb to spreading necrosis, and knowing that even with intervention, it was too late. The body could not be saved.

There was something of that same air of rot to the man from the Pickwell family. He was gaunt to the point of becoming almost cadaverous, with grayish skin and fingers that seemed a trifle too long, like they had been shaped by someone who didn't fully understand the way human bones were supposed to fit together.

His counterpart from the Latour family was no better. She was short and slight and somehow feral, with teeth that seemed too sharp and plentiful for her small, heavily lipsticked mouth, and hair that gave the impression of feathers stuck together by dried mud, or blood, or some terrible mixture of the two.

I hated them both on sight. It wasn't fair, and I was the last person who needed to be judging people based on appearances, but looking at them made something in the back of my brain start to itch, like it wanted me to get away while I still could.

Whatever signal I was picking up, I was the only one. Addison approached the pair with one hand outstretched and her best "I am in the business of doing business" smile on her face. "Mr. Pickwell, Ms. Latour, it's a pleasure to meet you both. I'm Addison Tanaka, and this is the rest of the Answer Squad."

A terrible name, but the dot-com had been available when we'd needed it, and it wasn't so on the nose as to lock us into a single segment of the "teen sleuths solve mysteries, try not to die horrible deaths" market.

"Thank you so much for agreeing to let us have a chance to unravel the mysteries of Spindrift House," continued Addison, not seeming to notice that our local contacts were looking at her like she was a charming oddity, something to be seen in a museum or a carnival show, but not in front of them in the real, material world. "I promise you, we're all going to come away from this experience satisfied."

"That seems very likely," said Mr. Pickwell. His voice was like rocks and gravel rolling over the bottom of a barrow, and a chill rushed over my skin, nearly forcing me to take a step backward. I shivered, stepping a little closer to Kevin.

No one seemed to notice. Ms. Latour smiled her toothy smile at Addison, and said, "We have the paperwork here for you to sign. Once that's done, we can call our team to examine your equipment and personal effects, and will be able to show you to the house. I assume you've gone over all relevant terms and conditions?"

"Yes, ma'am," said Addison. "They were quite clearly stated on your posting, and everything appears to be in order."

"It's like watching two really boring wizards try to stare each other down," muttered Kevin.

Normally I would have laughed, maybe punched him in the arm, and let the tension go. I couldn't do any of those things. All I could do was try to keep myself from shaking, and resist the urge to grab Addison by the arm and yell for her to run. There was no logical reason for me to be this revolted by two people who, while odd, were well within the standard range for the human race. If I'd seen one or even both of them in a grocery store or waiting in line at the movies, I wouldn't have thought twice. But here, now, with the sound of the sea roaring behind them like the beating of some huge, horrible heart...

The sea. I hadn't seen the sea since my parents had died, sending me to live by the shores of Lake Michigan, which had seemed, to my half-formed child's eyes, to be essentially the same thing. Here, now, standing within sight of the Atlantic, I finally understood that no lake, however mighty, however vast, could ever hope to compete.

Waves slammed into the shore, sending runnels of water through the streets of Port Mercy, and as they ran out again, chasing the tide, I thought I could hear words in the susurration of salt against sand. I thought I could hear it calling to me, like it remembered me, like it knew my name, and I thought—

"Harlowe." Addison sounded annoyed, snapping me out of my daze and forcing me to focus on her. She had somehow moved so that she was standing directly in front of me, leaving Mr. Pickwell and Ms. Latour alone beside the sign.

But that didn't make sense. They were in the middle of the negotiations, weren't they? Addison handled the paperwork, made sure the contracts were good, that everything was arranged to guarantee that we'd get paid on time and without any chance of getting stiffed. She'd never leave the conversation unfinished. Would she?

"Harley didn't sleep too good last night," said Kevin, coming to my rescue, as he always did. "I guess it's catching up with her."

"So drink a damn Pepsi," said Addison. "Don't zone out when we're meeting the clients."

"The clients?" I echoed.

"They want to be introduced to everyone, not just me, since we're all going into the house together." Addison scraped together a thin, artificial-looking smile. I managed, somehow, not to quail away.

"Right," I said instead, and followed her, along with Kevin and Andy, to the people who were hopefully going to sign our checks.

Mr. Pickwell shook hands with Kevin and Andy first, before turning his terrible attention on me. His eyes raked me up and down before he smiled, slowly, and offered me his hand.

"You must be Harlowe," he said. "Jones, wasn't it? That's a common name here in Maine, but I suppose that can't be where your people are from."

"Illinois," I said, fighting the urge to step back, away, out of reach. "Chicago area."

"This must be a big change from Lake Michigan," he said. Sensing that I wasn't going to close the last few inches between us, he did, folding his fingers over mine.

His skin was cold, as cold as the grave, and it was all I could do not to snatch my hand away and flee back to the car, where it was warm, and safe, and famil-iar. His smile widened, like he could somehow sense my discomfort, and found it both telling and delight-ful. He let me go, and I gasped despite myself, almost stumbling.

"It's a pleasure to meet you all," he said, and turned, nudging Ms. Latour aside before she could ask for a handshake of her own. "Let's finish that paperwork and get you all ready to meet the house, shall we?"

After everything else that had happened, the check of our persons and equipment was almost per-functory. Ms. Latour made a quick call and six more people appeared, a mixture of men and women, some with the pallor and hollow eyes of the Pickwells, oth-ers with the sharp, excessive brightness of the Latours. I was used to the concept of the family resemblance— I spent most of my waking hours with Andy and Addy, who were as alike as it was possible for non-identical twins to be—but I had also had people who didn't know the exact nature of my relationship to Kevin claim that we were "obviously" brother and sister, because he had my nose, or I had his ears. I had never seen "we just look like that" written so plainly and blatantly across so many faces.

Kevin and Andy supervised the search of our lug-gage and gear, standing by and watching without protest as six strangers ran their hands over everything we owned. If not literally, then spiritually: this was everything we owned that *mattered*. These were the tools of our trade, the fingerprint kits and cameras and yes, ghost-hunting equipment, because there's no such thing as being too prepared for what might happen.

Addison, meanwhile, was busy breaking down the minutiae of our contracts with Mr. Pickwell and Ms. Latour, who listened to her points and counterpoints with the mildly amused tolerance of adults listening to a very precocious child. Something about the way they looked at her made me uncomfortable, although I couldn't put my finger on quite why. Maybe it was the gleam in their eyes, or the predatory set to their shoulders…or maybe it was just that I needed to focus on something other than the sweet, beguiling whisper of the sea.

The sea. If I could just go closer, if I could let it run across my shoes and dip my fingers in it, I would—

I would nothing. I shook away the lingering compulsion and turned to see Andy and Kevin loading our things back into the trunk. If I'd lost time again, I hadn't lost much. Now, finally, it was time to see what we had driven all this way to see.

"If you would follow us," said Ms. Latour. She walked toward a gleaming white sedan of a model I didn't recognize. Mr. Pickwell followed her, sliding into the passenger seat as she got behind the wheel.

We returned to our car in uneasy silence, leaving the six assistants standing silent by the side of the road. I tried to remember whether I'd heard any of them say a word. They watched us drive away, and their eyes reflected the gleam of our brake lights, and I tore my eyes away from the mirror. I didn't want to see that. I didn't want to see any of this.

Ms. Latour drove slowly along the winding road that led from Port Mercy to Spindrift House. Fog began scudding across the pavement when we were less than halfway there, until Addison had to turn the headlights on just to see where we were going. Kevin put a hand on my knee, squeezing reassuringly. I didn't say anything.

And then there it was, looming out of the fog like an iceberg appearing without warning in the middle of the sea, like the enchanted cabin in a fairy tale: Spindrift House, standing straight and tall and surprisingly, confusingly solid, as if it had been constructed only hours ago, as if it had been waiting for us for a hundred years. Its windows stared blankly at the road that ran past its fence line, only to peter out and die some hundred yards farther along, where it met the end of the cliff.

Ms. Latour pulled over. Addison did the same. One by one, we got out of the car, turning our faces toward Spindrift House, seeking its silent majesty like flowers seek the sun.

"You have a week," said Ms. Latour. "We have cameras on the exterior of the property, of course; they'll know if you leave. Food can be delivered to the address on your paperwork, and one of our people will bring it the rest of the way up to the house. We're all very invested in your success."

"Yes," said Mr. Pickwell, who had somehow appeared beside her. "We wish you only the truest of answers."

"We won't let you down," said Addison.

She started for the house, her suitcase in one hand and her go-bag in the other. The rest of us, drawn by the jesses of long habit, followed her, and Spindrift House was waiting, door gaping wide, to swallow us down and begin the long, terrible process of digestion.

Part II:
Low Tide

Chapter 4:
The Consumed

1.

Nature abhors an angle.

Peace is found in the curve, in the spiral, in the soft, irregular shape of growth allowed to seek itself, unchecked, unrestrained. Stasis is an abomination unto the cosmos. A life is short but eternity is long: to stop, to cease, to even hesitate is to blaspheme against creation. There are so many forms to try, so many things to experience. How could any thinking creature want to limit themselves to the comfortable, the familiar, or the known?

The roots of Spindrift House dig deep into the earth, deeper than the foundations, deeper than the roots of the hill on which it perches, fat with secrets, like a brooding spider overlooking the tangled reaches of its web. They reach even beyond the foundations of the town, down into the place where the water waits. The ancient, unflinching sea. Spindrift House has always been here, will always be here, will outlast nations and continents, plucking at its web, trying, with all of its terrible might, to call the lost ones home.

I can hear it calling. I can hear it calling to me. Come home, it says. Come home, come home, come—

I woke with a start, sitting bolt upright in the chilly, silent room, clutching my sleeping bag against my chest. My heart was hammering so hard that it seemed to reverberate through my entire body, like a cloister bell calling the faithful in from the fields.

Dim moonlight trickled through the window, turning the room around me into a blurry field of variegated grays. I groped around on the nightstand until I found my glasses and shoved them onto my face. The blurs resolved themselves into heavy antique furniture, some still draped in the dust covers that had greeted us, like so many frozen ghosts, when we first stepped inside.

Shreds of dream still clung to me as I climbed off the bed. Off, not out: while the rooms we were using as our temporary homes were all fully furnished, I hadn't felt comfortable slipping between a dead person's sheets. Using their pillows was bad enough. I'd barely been able to bring myself to sleep in my own sleeping bag on top of the mattress. If we'd been able to be completely sure that there were no rats, I would probably have taken my chances with the floor.

There was no electricity in Spindrift House, at least not yet. The previous owners had wired the place sometime in the seventies, but the three families currently feuding over the land saw no point in paying the bills when the house was unoccupied. According to Addison, the power would be on by the morning. I wasn't sure about that. No matter how loudly money speaks, utilities tend to drag their feet. But I supposed we'd see.

My phone was on the nightstand, next to where my glasses had been. I picked it up, turned on the flashlight app, and carefully walked across the still-unfamiliar room to the door. If I was going to be awake, I might as well find something to do.

The smell of chocolate greeted me as soon as I stepped into the hall. I blinked, bemused, and sniffed again. The smell of dusty, unused rooms was still there, buried under the sweeter chocolatey perfume, but it was real. I was sure that it was real. I frowned a little and started following it, keeping my flashlight trained on the ground in front of me. The last thing I wanted to do was trip on some ancient rug and send my glasses flying.

It wasn't just the exterior of Spindrift House that was in surprisingly good condition. The inside looked like it could have been shut up at the end of the previous season, left to wait out the winter alone, with the promise of its residents returning in the spring. Every room was fully furnished, filled with heavy, expensive-looking pieces protected by oiled dust cloths that fell away at the slightest touch, as if they had just been waiting to show off their scarcely concealed treasures. Oil paintings and antique portraits hung on the walls, and while they weren't covered, their glass was barely smudged with dust and salt residue. It could have been the set of a period drama—or, as seemed somehow, shiveringly more likely, a horror movie.

IN THE Shadow OF Spindrift House

There were three first floor bedrooms, all of them arrayed along the same single hall. Kevin, Andy, and I had claimed them as soon as we'd finished carrying our gear inside, Andy because he wanted to be close to the kitchen, Kevin because he didn't want to be tempted to smoke indoors, and me because my eyesight and dark stairs were a bad combination. Addison had huffed, declared that she'd been missing her privacy anyway, and gone up to the second floor to find herself a place to sleep.

This was our home. For the next week, or however long it took us to prove who owned the house and who didn't, this was our home. It only made sense that we'd try to settle in, even if I would have preferred it a little—okay, more than a little—if we'd all stopped pretending to be brave and just set up a makeshift campground in the largest room we'd been able to find, the way we'd done for our first few overnight mysteries, back when we'd been little kids and no one had thought there was anything untoward about our sleeping arrangements.

All that had changed when we were in the ninth grade and unraveled the mystery of the supposed banshee haunting an abandoned movie theater near Addison and Andy's house. I'd only been living with

Kevin for a few months at that point, and he and I had a tendency to fall asleep slumped together like puppies, me reassuring myself that he really wanted me there, him reassuring himself that his new sister hadn't vanished in the night like one of our ghosts. Andy and Addy had still been in the habit of sharing everything, from sneakers to sleeping bags. After we'd discovered that the "banshee" was just a disgruntled camera operator, the local paper had swept in to do what they called a human interest piece, and what Kevin's mom had called a hatchet job.

They'd taken pictures of the four of us, something we were already used to. And, for the first time, they'd taken pictures of what Addison had proudly called our "home base," focusing on how close together the sleeping bags were—how two of them were zipped together, and neither of those was mine. Maybe the adults who'd taken the pictures and written the story had honestly been trying to show how organized and professional we'd been, even at that young age. Maybe. But for our classmates, seeing four sleeping bags piled together like that, so that any one of us could reach out and touch any of the others, reassuring ourselves of their presence, the scene had sung a different song:

Perverts.

Kevin and I hadn't gotten it quite as badly as Andy and Addy. We weren't blood siblings, after all, and some of the boys had still been under the impression that Kevin had encouraged his mother to take me in so he could try and peep when I was in the shower. But Andy and Addy had always been inseparable, had always been a united front, and now, for the first time, there was a potential gap in their armor.

It hadn't worked completely—I don't think anything ever could have, not with those two. They still shared motel rooms when we were on the road, still looked for each other before they did anything else. But when we were officially "on the job," in any sort of situation that might call for professional documentation, Addison made it a point to sleep as far away from the rest of us as possible.

Sometimes I think it's a good thing that I'm too afraid of prison to go around punching people, or my list would be a mile long and my knuckles would be perennially bruised.

The hall ended in a kitchen large enough to cook dinner for a dozen people, with a vaulted ceiling that played host to not one, not two, but three large skylights. Moonlight flooded the room. In case that wasn't enough, candles in jam jars were set up on the counters, table, and butcher's block, filling the room with a sweet, flickering luminescence. Andy was standing by the stove in sweatpants and a hoodie, stirring a pan of what I could only assume was hot cocoa.

I smiled as I leaned up against the doorway. Andy was the quiet one, the one who liked rules and patterns and doing the right thing, and sometimes people assumed that out of all of us, he was the one who didn't carry his weight. They couldn't have been more wrong. He just did his part in subtler ways. I found the messes, Kevin made them worse, Addison charged in to beat down whatever happened to be standing on our way, and Andy came along behind with a broom and dustpan. Take any one of us away and we ceased to function.

"Couldn't sleep?" I asked.

"Slept plenty in the car," said Andy. "They turned off the electricity and left the gas on. Maybe they were hoping the house would burn down and they'd be able to get on with selling the land."

"Maybe," I said agreeably. Andy was soothing. Always had been. Sometimes I wished I liked boys, just because Andy was so soothing. Life would have been a lot easier if I'd been in love with him. "Is there enough for me?"

Andy looked over his shoulder, flashing me one of his rare smiles. "There's enough for everyone. I didn't know if anyone would be able to sleep when we're all standing at the gateway to such a big mystery. Marshmallows in yours?"

"Please." I walked over and took a seat at the kitchen table, which was solid oak and would have been the pride of any modern hipster's house. The candlelight made the subtle patterns in the wallpaper waver and dance, mermaids waltzing slowly with strange deep-sea fish. I touched one of them with my fingertips, and was almost surprised when it wasn't damp.

"I have biscotti, too, although I can't warm them at all until the electricity comes on," said Andy, setting a mug of cocoa in front of me. Five marshmallows floated on the surface, already starting to lose cohesion.

I picked it up, took a sip, and blinked in surprise. "This is real milk."

"Yeah." Andy favored me with a second smile. "I still had some in the cooler. With no fridge, it was going to go off pretty fast, and what better way to go than becoming cocoa?"

"You are a saint among men." I took another sip. The cocoa was hot and sweet and rich, coating my tongue in a syrupy film and warming my stomach from the inside. I'd be able to sleep again after this. I was sure of it.

"I try." He sat down on the other side of the table, cradling his own mug between his hands. "Kevin went outside to smoke. He says he doesn't like the air inside the house."

"Doesn't like the air?" I frowned. "It's not nearly as stale as I'd expected it to be. Dusty, sure, but we've been in places that were way dustier, and most of those *stank*. Remember the bowling alley? The one where there were supposedly alligators in the basement?"

Andy wrinkled his nose. "I wish it had been alligators. Alligators would have been a lot more pleasant."

"Agreed." I took another sip of my cocoa. "I could do with never having to see another cannibal cult again."

"Yeah." Andy frowned, giving me a thoughtful look. "You can't smell it? Really?"

"Smell what?"

"This house. It's like..." He stopped for a moment, clearly reaching for words, before he finally said, "It's like it's rotting from the inside out. Like it's been sick for a long, long time, and somehow it's managed not to let it show, but it can't keep pretending for much longer. It smells like low tide in here, Harley. It smells like the entire ocean getting ready to crash down on our heads. You really can't *tell?*"

I stared at him, trapped somewhere midway between confused and appalled. "No," I said. "I can't. It just smells like another house to me. Dusty, and we should probably open a few windows, but it's not... anything like what you're describing. It's not bad."

The kitchen door opened and closed while Andy was still trying to formulate a reply. "Ooh, cocoa!" said Kevin. His voice had that bright, distanced note it always took on when he was well and truly baked. "Can I have some?"

"I made enough for everyone," said Andy.

"Cool," said Kevin. "Hey, did you know there's a little family graveyard behind the house?" He ladled cocoa into a mug as he continued, "There's the road in the front, and then there's the end of the cliff to the right and all that land that I guess comes with the house to the left, and then if you go walking behind, you'll find a whole bunch of old tombstones and markers. We should go check them out more in daylight. Some of them are still legible."

"If they say who's buried there, it might be a clue," said Andy.

Kevin shook his head as he joined us at the table. "Nah. I mean, I thought of that, because it's super obvious, and sometimes that means nobody caught it, you know?"

We all laughed, wryly. One of the first things we'd learned as pre-teen detectives had been that sometimes people—meaning adults—were so fixated on the idea of a mystery that they overlooked the things that were right in front of their noses.

Sobering, Kevin continued, "But I saw headstones with 'Upton,' and 'Latour,' and even 'Pickwell' on them, and they were all right near the edge of the yard. Even if people were in love with the idea of a mystery, I don't think the families who've been fighting over this house would overlook something that obvious. The answer probably isn't in the graveyard, or if it is, it isn't in the way we think."

"Still worth looking into," said Andy. "I'll go out with a camera tomorrow."

"Oh, thank God, cocoa." Addison appeared in the kitchen doorway, uncharacteristically rumpled, digging the heel of one hand into her eye. "Is *anyone* getting any sleep?"

"Nope," I said cheerfully. "Welcome to the party."

"You are all spiteful, spiteful creatures," she said, and made her way to the stove.

We sat up for hours after that, drinking cocoa, talking, laughing at one another's ideas about where to start unraveling the mystery of Spindrift House, and if I'd ever been happier, I couldn't remember it. It was a perfect night, as long as I could close my ears, and my heart, to the distant, ceaseless sighing of the sea.

2.

The power came on just before noon.

We'd already eaten by that point, eggs scrambled with cheese over the gas stove, which was quickly becoming Andy's favorite thing about the house, and Kevin and I had spent several hours slogging around the graveyard and the grounds, taking pictures of things that could be photographed and writing down our impressions of things that couldn't be.

Some of the grave markers were...disturbing. My family name appeared as often as the Pickwells and Latours, which might have seemed like proof that I was in the right place, if I hadn't been so repulsed by everything else about the stones. Most of the dead were either under the age of five or over the age of eighty. There were none of the angels or cherubs I would have expected for so many infant graves: instead, they were marked with tiny skulls, or with what I thought might be nautilus shells, spiraling and many-chambered and somehow terrible. And the epitaphs...

I didn't want to think about the epitaphs if I didn't have to.

Kevin and I were walking back toward the house when the windows suddenly lit up bright as day, and we heard Andy shouting. We broke into a run at the same time, and I barely beat him to the back door, slamming it open.

Andy was in the kitchen, turning off appliances while the garbage disposal—who would have thought this ancient pile of wood and stone would have a *garbage disposal?*—roared to itself in the sink. I darted across the room and flicked it off. Andy shot me a grateful look, while Kevin continued deeper into the house, presumably to start flipping switches and preventing something worse from happening.

"Whoever was here last left everything on, even though the power wasn't," Andy said. "If I didn't know better, I'd say they really *were* trying to burn the place down."

I frowned. "That's what you said last night, about the gas."

"I did, and I stand by it." He frowned at the blender, which had apparently offended him in some way. "This isn't how you shutter a house. I understand turning things off when no one's living here, but you have to be methodical about it. You have to make sure one blown fuse doesn't spell the end of your real estate investment."

He rubbed at the back of his neck with one hand as he spoke, a nervous tic that had stayed with him since childhood. Addison used to do the same thing when we were younger, until that rigid self-control of hers had kicked in and she had begun the ruthless, relentless elimination of anything someone else could look at and consider a weakness.

"You all right?" I asked.

Andy shook his head. "Just confused by this place. That's all. Nothing about it makes sense. It's in amazing repair, and there have been owners who didn't belong to the three families laying claim—how does that work? Did someone sell it when they didn't have the legal right to do so? If that's the case, shouldn't there be records that can be used to track initial provenance? What happened to the most recent owner or owners?"

"I can answer that," said Addison. We turned. She was standing in the kitchen doorway, a tablet in one hand, flicking her fingers across its surface in a quick, almost dismissive rhythm, like the files she'd downloaded before we moved outside of wireless range had somehow been naughty. "The house is entailed."

I blinked. Andy blinked. I recovered first.

"Entailment doesn't happen in the United States," I said. "That's an archaic British concept."

"Yes, but once upon a time, the colonies were an archaic British concept, and while entailment is rare in the modern world, and not legal in most places, there are four states that still allow it." Addison offered me a grim smile. "Massachusetts, Delaware, Rhode Island, and take a wild guess."

"Maine," said Andy.

"Good guess," said Addison. "It's *difficult* to entail an estate, and it takes a lot of very confusing paperwork, but someone in the past of this house was apparently very fond of confusing paperwork. Like, sexual fetish levels of fond. Near as I can tell, it was a compromise between the three families. They all thought that by the time the new 'owner' passed away and the estate reverted, they'd have figured out who actually owned the place."

"I'm guessing that didn't happen, since we're here," I said.

Addison nodded. "They allowed the house to go through a sale that was honestly more of a long-term lease, given the entailment, and kept trying to figure out who actually owned it. They'd done this little trick before, several times, and I guess they didn't anticipate any trouble."

She paused in the way that always meant she wanted someone to ask her for more details. I knew my part in this little production.

"What went wrong?" I asked.

"The most recent owner filed a motion to have the entailment dismissed, on the grounds that there was no clear line of ownership, which made the contract technically illegal," said Addison. "They made it pretty far through the process before they disappeared with no legal heirs and no family to take up the fight. Since no one was paying the lawyers, and the Pickwell and Latour families, at least, are more than equipped to squash most attempts at getting in their way, the case was dropped and the house has not been placed back on the market since."

"Disappeared?" asked Andy.

"In the middle of the night," said Addison. "Left everything behind. Car, computer, clothing—even ID and credit cards. There was some concern about foul play, but again, no family. No evidence. It was all swept under the rug."

"Or out to sea," I murmured.

Addison shot me a look. "What?"

"Nothing." I shook my head. "So I guess he left everything turned on before he went off to become a missing person? That seems weird. Why didn't whoever came to close up the house turn things off before they shut off the electricity?"

"That isn't the mystery that gets us paid," said Addison.

"No, but it's the mystery that's going to make me wish I'd brought a *lot* more pot." Kevin appeared behind her, looking genuinely unsettled. "Have any of you been up to the attic yet?"

"I wasn't going to go up there with the power out," said Addison. "Seemed like a good way to get a broken ankle."

"Probably smart," said Kevin. "I think you should come up there now."

The three of us in the kitchen exchanged a bewildered look. Then, with a staggered set of shrugs, we turned to follow him to the stairs.

Andy flipped off the kitchen lights as he stepped into the hall, and that narrow slice of Spindrift House was cast into darkness once again.

3.

We trooped up the stairs the way we always had, ever since we were children: Kevin in the front, with Addison walking close behind him, me behind her, and Andy bringing up the rear, a position that had led to him being taken hostage several times when we were teenagers, snatched by criminals with more guts than sense who'd assumed that if they could incapacitate one of our boys, they'd be in a better position to incapacitate the rest of us. Andy had never fought them, just sat back and let himself be tied to a chair, or a support beam, or whatever was handy, and waited to watch his sister kick their asses.

Maybe we were all a little too comfortable in our roles, using them as situational security blankets that meant we didn't have to take anything too seriously. No matter how bad things got, we knew what we were supposed to do. Kevin led us into danger, seemingly keeping Addison from being the first at risk, while actually putting her in a position to jerk him to safety if necessary. Andy and I kept our distance. Everything was as it was meant to be.

Nothing was as it was meant to be. I just didn't know it yet.

As we walked, I sniffed the air as unobtrusively as I could, trying to find that rotten smell that Andy had mentioned. It wasn't there. All I smelled was dust, and the sweet, almost comforting decay of old fabric, which had to be coming from the velvety wallpaper covering the walls to all sides. It's a smell that lingers in almost all homes over a certain age. Kevin's house has that smell. So did my grandparents' house, back when I believed I could be safe there. I couldn't imagine anyone breathing that in and feeling like they needed to flee.

"Do you smell it?" asked Andy, sounding almost hopeful.

I shook my head.

"Huh," he said, and said nothing more after that, as we followed Kevin along the third floor hallway and to the narrow, unmarked wooden door that hid the attic steps.

They were narrow and rickety, the first things in Spindrift House that looked like they could use more than a good dusting. Something was structurally wrong with them; the wood seemed almost to *squish* underfoot, like it was considering falling apart entirely. The banister was slick under my fingers, damp with some scentless, unspeakable fluid.

Maybe not scentless. Addison lifted her fingers to her nose, sniffed them, and made an offended gagging sound. "You'd think millionaires could afford to buy some air freshener," she said, voice prim. "Cover your mouths. If this is fungal, it could be a lawsuit waiting to happen."

Kevin already had his hand over his mouth. Andy was breathing shallowly, like he wanted to take in as little of the air in the stairwell as possible. And I...

I didn't see the problem. I sniffed my own fingers, trying to be unobtrusive about it. They smelled perfectly normal. Whatever everyone else was finding in this house, it wasn't there for me.

We reached the top of the stairs before I could decide what, if anything, I wanted to say about the situation, and stepped into the vast, cluttered expanse of the attic. It seemed too large for the house below us, like it had been grafted on from someplace even bigger, built according to an even more grandiose design. The eaves were too high above our heads. The angles of the windows were wrong.

I stopped in the doorway, trying not to lose my balance as the room stretched and bent around me. Andy's hands were suddenly on my shoulders. I turned and blinked at him, and barely managed not to recoil. He looked suddenly unfamiliar, almost alien, like he and I had come from such different ecosystems that my eyes were trying to deny the reality of his presence.

"Harley?" His voice was as strange as the rest of him, distant and distorted. "Are you okay?"

"I…" I stopped, struggling to find room in my lungs for another breath. Then I sagged, and Andy's arms were there to hold me up, keeping me from crashing to the floor.

"Get a window!" he barked.

Kevin and Addison hurried to comply. There was a scrape and a creak as Kevin forced the nearest window open. It was followed by a banging sound, like someone had opened a door.

The smell of the sea rushed in through the openings, and I could breathe again. I sagged against Andy for a few more seconds before I cautiously straightened up, testing the stability of my legs. They seemed willing to hold me, and when I breathed, my lungs inflated easily, with none of the strange resistance I had encountered before.

"Harlowe?" I turned toward the sound of Addison's voice. She was as familiar as she had ever been, best and most beloved of friends. She was also frowning, a speculative expression on her face. "What just happened?"

"I don't know," I said. "It was like the room was moving."

"Uh-huh." She suddenly thrust her hand in my face, fingers beneath my nose. "Can you smell this?"

I sniffed obediently before shaking my head. "Just the soap you used the last time you washed your hands."

"Okay. Okay." She took a step back, running one hand through her hair. "There's a bad smell downstairs that you don't notice at all; it's worse on the stairs to the attic, and you still can't smell it, but when we get you up here, it's like there's no air. Does that sound about right?"

"Yes," I said slowly. Then my eyes widened. "You don't think—"

"I do," she said. "Gas leak."

"We have to get out of here," I said. "Gas isn't a toy."

"We *can't*." The look Addison gave me then was a perfect blend of frustration and disgust, like all this had somehow become my fault. "We signed a contract, remember? If we leave the property for any reason, we can't come back."

Andy looked alarmed. "That can't be right. There must be an exception for health and safety."

"There's not," said Addison. "If we leave because we're afraid there's a gas leak, that's it; we're done. They won't let us come back for another shot. Too much chance we could have used this as an opportunity to case the joint and plant evidence that we'll 'coincidentally' find when we come back. They won't pay for fuel or lodging. They won't give us an opportunity to explain. We'll come out of this worse than we went in."

"Then we can't leave." It took me a moment to realize that I was the one who had spoken. I straightened, pulling away from Andy, and pushed doggedly on. "Gas isn't a joke, but we can work around it. We keep the windows open, we set alarms, and we sleep in shifts. That's more productive anyway, since it means someone is always awake and searching the house for clues. If things don't improve, we go back to our traveling sleeping arrangements."

Addison looked unhappy about that, but she didn't argue, which was the next best thing to wholehearted acceptance, coming from her.

Kevin moved back into view, somehow managing to project excitement and concern at the same time. "If we're not leaving, you should come and take a look at this," he said, and beckoned us deeper into the attic.

There was no reason not to follow him. The scent of the sea was continuing to pour in through the open window, and I was feeling more stable all the time—something that was helped as Andy moved to open another window, and another, until the attic was filled with sweet sea air. Addison and I exchanged a glance, and let Kevin lead us across the attic to a wide set of double doors that had been pushed open and hooked into place, providing a perfectly rectangular slice of New England sky.

It was slate gray swirled with streaks of palest blue, breaking through between the clouds. I started to take a step forward, one hand raised, like I thought I could touch the sky itself, like it would tell me all its secrets. Addison grabbed my wrist, stopping me. I turned to blink at her, bemused.

"Careful," she said. "You're still shaky."

She didn't sound like she thought I was shaky. She sounded suspicious, almost, like she didn't understand why I was doing what I was doing, and didn't approve of it. I held her gaze for a count of ten, trying to understand.

In the end, I was the one who looked away, still confused. Addison let go of my wrist.

"Is that the widow's walk?" she asked.

"Uh-huh," said Kevin. "I knew the door had to be up here, and it seemed like the fastest way to let a whole lot of air into the room at once. You okay, Harley? Not dizzy anymore?"

"I'm great," I said, and mustered a wan smile as I moved toward him. This time, Addison didn't stop me, and I stepped out onto the widow's walk and stopped, unable to move any farther, unable to even breathe.

Before me spread the Atlantic in all its power and glory, a shining sheet of black water stretching from one end of the horizon to the other. Ripples of foam danced across its surface, whitecaps lifting and falling with the waves. Seagulls circled overhead, and their cries were strange poetry, filled with secrets human ears would never untangle, woven layer on layer into the hidden world before me.

My knees felt like they were going to buckle. I grabbed the railing, still staring at the sea.

"It's beautiful, isn't it?" Kevin stepped up next to me. "I mean, this sort of thing makes me understand why people would come live in the middle of nowhere like this. It's the view. Look, you can see the graveyard from here."

I followed his finger to the patch behind the house. Seen from above, there was no rhyme or reason to the burial plots; they were simply tossed in wherever they would fit, like toys nobody wanted anymore. It was oddly akin to the attic, with its piles of junk and—presumably—treasures heaped up indiscriminately, like nothing had any more value than anything else.

"This isn't what you brought us up here to see, is it?"

Kevin's face fell. Whatever reaction he'd wanted, it hadn't been that. "No. Come on back this way."

He stepped away from the rail, heading back toward the attic. I stayed where I was for a few more seconds. I wanted to stay forever. This, here, this was perfect. The wind in my hair, the smell of the sea in my nostrils...perfect.

"Coming?"

I wrenched my eyes away from the sea with an effort none of them would ever understand and turned to follow Kevin inside.

Andy and Addison had already found what he wanted to show us: a leather-bound photo album, each page covered in a yellowing plastic sheet. Addison had produced a piece of tissue from somewhere and was using it to protect her fingers as she delicately turned the pages. I caught a glimpse of Spindrift House, black and white and imposing, and—

"Hey!" I blurted, rushing forward. "Stop there. Look."

Addison stopped. Wordlessly, the four of us clustered around the book and looked at the photograph in front of us.

IN THE Shadow OF Spindrift House

Like so many of the others, it centered on Spindrift House, casting the manse as the most important part of the shot, like without it, there would be no point in taking a picture. Four people stood in front of it, two men and two women. One of the men and one of the women were dressed almost identically, in sensible clothes and running shoes; their hair was black, their expressions similar. The other man had brown hair and a scraggly beard and the general air of someone who had dressed himself in the dark and was, under the circumstances, quite pleased with himself.

The fourth person was me.

Not perfectly so, but so close that if I hadn't already known what my mother looked like, I would have assumed I was holding proof that she had been here before me. The woman in the picture's hair was calmer than my frizzy mess, and she wasn't wearing glasses; she looked at the world without filters. But her mouth was mine, and the line of her nose, and even the faintly defeated slope of her shoulders. She was dressed roughly, in plain trousers and a button-up shirt, and looked like she belonged to another era, something more modern than the frozen world around her.

"Whoa," said Kevin.

"Yeah," I agreed, brushing my fingers across the plastic covering the image, like I thought I could somehow blur it or wipe it away. Nothing changed. My own eyes kept looking at me out of a photograph taken before I was born, and the room was spinning again, for reasons that had nothing to do with the quality of the air.

"We already knew the Uptons were historically involved with the house," said Addison. "This just proves that one of your ancestors was here."

I lifted my head and blinked at her. "She looks *exactly like me.*"

"She doesn't." Addison stuck her chin out stubbornly, refusing to be budged. "She has better hair. Sometimes I wonder if you even know how to use a brush."

Addison could be cruel when she was uncomfortable. That was a fact of life, as ordinary and expected as "Kevin is anxious" and "Andy will feed us." It still stung. I'd never been sure whether or not she knew how deeply in love with her I was, but having her attack my personal appearance never failed to hurt.

"We should look to see whether there's any more evidence of the Upton family here in the attic," I said.

"Maybe there's a false bottom in one of these old wardrobes or something."

There wasn't.

There were spiders—so many spiders, spiders without number, which meant legs that were even more without number, until my skin felt like it was going to crawl off my body and join their arachnid army—and there were tiny, darting silverfish, like sardines of the land, and there was dust that clogged the air and made me even more grateful for the open windows, but there were no secret compartments or hidden safes. There were just racks of ancient, fragile clothing, and boxes filled with mementos of lives that had never, up until this moment, come anywhere close to ours.

Subdued, we went back downstairs. Andy cut spaghetti into makeshift straws, and we drew to see who would be sleeping when. Addison and I got the first shift, and I went to my room alone, feeling more lost—more orphaned—than I had in years.

Spindrift House sighed around me, and everything was still.

Chapter 5:

Leaking

1.

Her name was Violet Upton, and she was the daughter of one of the richest fishermen in Port Mercy. The man she had married was Lyall Upton, her third cousin, and if there had been some whispers in the town about how her last name hadn't changed when her belly started to swell, she could ignore them. She had the finest house, the finest husband, and would soon have the finest child in all of New England. At night, she slept with her window open, listening to the sweet, distant singing of the sea.

It had been calling her home since she was only a child, but now, for a time, it had changed the whisper of its words, urging her to stay on the land a little longer, to stay dry, to step away from the tangle of the tide. There was an ocean in her belly, one with its own strange customs and shadowy depths, and the two waters were never intended to meet. She would bear this child on the land, and any other children who came after it, until her child-bearing days were done, either out of age or illness. She knew that, as surely as she knew the tempo of the tides that surged within her, the beating of the second heart that slowly strengthened beneath her own.

The ocean was older than she was, older than her husband, older even than the delightful playground of Spindrift House, where every room was another sweet surprise. The ocean would wait. For now, she would be the captain of the ship that was her body, and she would see her single passenger safely to the shallow waters where life could thrive.

Violet walked the halls of Spindrift House, and she was not afraid, not even when she felt the windows watching her, not even when the wallpaper changed. She was a small predator in the protection of a larger one, and she was beloved, not only here, but fathoms below, in the dark and dreadful depths where she would one day be made glorious, where she would one day be made free.

This was a special day. Her man had brought her papers, bills of sale and ledgers proving that their family wealth was growing, and it was on her shoulders to keep them safe from those greedy hands that would snatch them away, leave the Uptons without their fair share of the ocean's bounty. She carried her precious burden through the house to the pantry door, and then, stepping through, pushed a certain shelf that caused the entire wall to swing inward, revealing the steps down to the basement. It smelled, deliciously, of decay.

She took the first step down—

"Harlowe! Snap out of it!"

Hands grabbed my shoulders, shocking me out of my fugue. For a heart-stopping moment, it felt like I was hanging suspended in darkness, looking down a terrible tunnel from which not even air could escape. I gasped, and the tunnel became a doorway, and the darkness became the ordinary shadows of an unlit hall.

Then Kevin was jerking me back, spinning me around so that his wide, terrified eyes were locked on mine. "Are you okay now? Are you awake?"

I blinked. I've never been a sleepwalker, but from the way he was looking at me... "I'm fine," I said. "I... was I asleep?"

"If you weren't, we're leaving right now, and screw the money." Kevin dug his fingers deeper into my shoulders, keeping me from pulling away as he searched my face. "You're the only sister I've got, and I don't even like my brother, so I'm not letting you die because this stupid house doesn't have its OSHA certification."

"Addison won't like that," I said, and winced, recognizing too late that it had been the exact wrong approach.

Kevin let go, looking at me disgustedly. "Addison can cope," he said. "If she wants to stay here and risk *her* brother, she can. Whatever. But I'm not risking you."

"I'm all right." I took a deep breath. The air was tinged with an oddly organic, fungal taste that hadn't been there before. Kevin looked dubious. I struggled to find a smile. "Really, I am. I was sleepwalking."

"Sleepwalking."

"Yeah."

"You don't sleepwalk."

"Not at home. But this place…my ancestors lived here. You saw that picture the same as I did. My blood family might have built this house. I'm on edge, everything is strange, and I'm sleepwalking. That's all."

Kevin's dubiousness didn't change. But he didn't grab me again, and I knew that he was listening. He loved a good mystery as much as the rest of us did, even if he was far more worried about the possible outcomes. "This better be the only time. If it doesn't stop, we're leaving."

"It's going to stop. It already has." I took a deep breath and looked over my shoulder at the dark tunnel that had been waiting to swallow me when Kevin snapped me out of my fugue.

It was a door. A door concealed behind the pantry shelves, designed to swing smoothly out when the correct piece was tugged, fitting perfectly into the available space. It hadn't been on any of the blueprints. There was no way I could have known that it was there.

Cool air was flowing up from the stairwell I'd revealed, filling the whole room with that delightful, faintly fungal scent.

"Harley?" said Kevin, voice gone suddenly very small.

"Yeah," I said, and took a step forward before I caught myself. "We need flashlights. Do you have a flashlight?"

He looked at me like I'd just said something totally ridiculous. "We need the others. I'm not going down there alone."

I wanted to point out that he wouldn't be alone: he'd be with me, and we were never alone when we were together. I didn't say anything. I was trying to deal with the acid ball of anger growing in my stomach, which didn't want me to share this new discovery with anyone. Certainly not with Addison, who seemed so determined to reduce the mysteries of Spindrift House to coincidences and gas leaks, like turning yet another ghost into a man in a mask. I loved her, but she made me so *mad* sometimes.

This was *my* family's house. We might not be able to prove it yet, but I knew it anyway, all the way down to the bottom of my bones. Uptons had lived and died within these walls for generations, and we had never once questioned the mystery of it all, or the magic of the living, breathing sea.

IN THE Shadow OF Spindrift House

Once again, Kevin's hand on my shoulder snapped me out of my fugue. "Harley?" he said, voice tight and anxious. He needed one of his special cookies. He needed *something* to take the edge off.

I knew how seriously he took our work. People liked to dismiss him as just another stoner, but there was no way he'd reach for the edibles, not now, not when we'd discovered a hidden stairwell down into the depths of the house—one that none of the other mystery seekers were likely to have found, which meant it might be the answer we'd been looking for. This was when the beginning ended, and the ending began. He'd stay clear-headed and terrified until it was safe for him to be something else, no matter how much it hurt him.

I might be annoyed by the idea of asking Addison along on this next part of our adventure, but I wasn't annoyed at Kevin. I never could have been. He was my brother, and I loved him too completely for that.

"I don't want to leave you here," he said uncomfortably. "I'm really sorry, I know how that sounds, but... the gas, and now the sleepwalking, and I'm just afraid that if you're the one who stays here, I'll come back and you'll be gone. So can you go get Andy and Addison, and I'll promise to stay right here, at the top of the stairs, and not go down into the dark without you, not even a little?"

I wanted to argue. I wanted to say that no, I wouldn't walk away and leave him alone with *my* mystery, *my* heritage. But he looked so hopeful, and we had been a team since the first time he'd been brave enough to sit down next to me and ask for my help. Silly, anxious Kevin, with his chickens and his callused hands and his heart big enough to hold the entire world.

"Sure," I said, and kissed his cheek before I turned and left him there alone.

Finding Andy was easy. He was up in the attic, flipping through a steamer chest filled with old papers and older photographs. As always, he came when I called.

Finding Addison was equally easy. She was still tucked into her borrowed bed, covers up around her chin, eyes closed, and she was beautiful—she had always been beautiful—and looking at her made the bitter thing under my breastbone twitch and writhe, remembering the way she'd dismissed the picture in the attic, the way she'd announced that we were going to put mysteries aside and move into something new, something that didn't want me. I still loved her. But in the moment, I hated her as well.

"Addison." I grabbed her shoulder and shook briskly. She opened her eyes.

"Harley?" Squinting, she sat up in bed, the covers falling away to reveal the old T-shirt she always slept in when we were on the road. She said lacy night-gowns were an invitation to abduction, and I couldn't really argue. "What are you doing in my room? Did something happen?"

Lacy nightgowns would also have been an invitation to short-circuiting my ability to form coherent thoughts. I might have slipped and told her I was having weird dreams and losing my temper, if she'd been wearing a lacy nightgown. But I'd seen her T-shirt before, and so I was able to swallow my babble and my bile in a single unsatisfying gulp before I said, "We found a door in the pantry. Kevin wanted all of us together before we went through it."

Just like that, all the mystery was gone. *I* hadn't found a door: we had. I hadn't seen it in a dream and followed the footsteps of a long-dead ancestor to the proper place: Kevin and I had just stumbled across the right clues, the right levers, as if they'd been waiting for us. This was perfectly ordinary, perfectly respectable.

How I hated thinking of the situation like that. But Addison's eyes lit up as she pushed the blankets aside and slid out of the bed, her feet finding the slippers she had set out and waiting as if she'd been waking up in this room every day of her life.

"All right, then, let's go," she said. "Mystery's waiting for us!" Then she paused, squinting at me in clear confusion. "Harlowe?"

"What?"

"Where are your glasses?"

2.

Andy had rigged a makeshift eye test in the kitchen, stacking boxes, cans, and books on the counter in descending order of text size. I was seated at the kitchen table, as far from the test as possible without leaving the room.

"Read the top line," he said.

"This is silly." I glared at him. "We're wasting time when we should be exploring the basement."

"Harley, peoples' eyes don't just *get better* in the middle of the night," said Kevin. He sounded, as always, genuinely concerned. It was like he thought I couldn't survive without him worrying about me. "The basement's a mystery that can wait. It's waited for decades. If your eyes are a sign that something's medically wrong—"

"If a gas leak was enough to improve a person's vision, people would stage them all the time," I said. "It's cheaper than Lasik."

No one laughed. Addison actually frowned.

"Read," she said.

I sighed, and said, "Top row is…yellow corn, hash, applesauce. Second row is…navy beans, tomatoes, ham—who even has canned ham? That's disgusting."

"Focus," said Kevin.

"Fine," I huffed. "Third row is lima beans, eel—yuck—and Irish stew. Did you find all this in the pantry? Who leaves this much food in the pantry of a house where no one lives? Don't eat *any* of that, you'll die. This is a lousy way to die."

The others were staring at me.

"What?"

"Harley…you just read every one of those cans." Kevin pointed at the counter, like I might have somehow missed the labels I'd just read aloud. "You're not wearing your glasses, and you just read *every one* of those cans. That's not possible. We need to get you to a doctor. You need to—this isn't right, this isn't *healthy*."

"I think her eyes getting better is sort of the definition of healthy," said Andy slowly. "If her vision was getting worse, that would be different, but…this is weird. That doesn't make it dangerous."

"And remember, we can't leave," said Addison. "If we go outside, we give up the money."

"I'd rather see the basement than a doctor," I protested, and finally stood. "Come on. I'm not the mystery. The house is the mystery."

"Right," said Kevin, looking at me sidelong. "The house."

We left the cans on the counter as we trooped toward the pantry, falling into a slightly different order as Addison took the lead. She shot me a few more irritated looks before pulling out one of our flashlights, clicking it on, and starting down the stairs.

"She's just worried about you," said Kevin, clearly trying to play the role of peacemaker. Normally, that would have been my job. Normally, I wasn't one of the people choosing sides. "You know, being in this house has all of us a little on edge."

"Yeah, okay," I said. He followed Addison down, and I followed him, while Andy, as always, brought up the rear.

The banister was damp and faintly sticky to the touch, like it had been dipped in something unspeakable and hadn't quite had enough time to dry. Curious, I touched the wall, which was smooth stone, probably an extension of the house foundations. It was dry. When I pulled my fingers away, a small waft of that sweet fungal smell followed, like even the stone had somehow figured out the way to rot.

Kevin turned his flashlight toward the ceiling, which was low and showed no evidence of having been wired for electricity. He made a faint noise of displeasure, and we kept on traveling down, deeper and deeper, until it felt like we must have walked halfway back to Port Mercy, like our next step would find us in brackish water up to our ankles.

"We have ground," called Addison, stepping off the stairs and onto a smooth, level floor. I squinted at it, trying to figure out what it was made of as Kevin followed her down. It looked like oiled dirt, which would make it older than anything else in the house. However ancient Spindrift House really was, this basement predated it by years, if not decades.

The air was dry. Whatever else might happen here, we weren't going to drown.

"There's a desk over here." Addison walked toward the far wall, flashlight raised high, steps careful. "It looks old."

"Who'd want to carry a desk down all those stairs?" asked Kevin.

No one, I thought, and knew, instinctively, that I was right. No one had carried that desk down the stairs. The stairs had been carved once the desk was where it needed to be, providing access to some essential piece of the puzzle we were now struggling to solve.

We shouldn't be here, I thought, and *I have been on my way here since the day I was born,* I thought, and those two seemingly contradictory concepts didn't contradict at all. They were the two sides of the same coin, both correct, both complete. We weren't supposed to be here. I knew that as surely as I knew that my glasses were sitting, unneeded, on the table next to my bed. But I had been coming here for so long, never really knowing it, never understanding what, or why, was calling me toward the unseen horizon.

This had been inevitable.

Addison had reached the desk. She let the beam of her flashlight play across it, picking out details, drawing out the moment. There was a smirk on her face, turned eerie and unkind by the flashlight's glow. She looked like a pirate preparing to plunder something that wasn't hers, that had never been meant for her, and my hands balled involuntarily into fists, preparing for a fight that wasn't coming.

I glanced down at them in surprise. I've never been a violent person, and this was *Addison*, my childhood crush turned adult infatuation, the woman I had told Kevin more than once—in private, and under the influence of alcohol—that I would be willing to die for, if the situation demanded it. One little smirk shouldn't have been enough to set me off.

"The wood seems to be solid and unaffected by the damp," said Addison.

Damp? What damp? My frown deepened, my hands unclenching. The basement was dry as a bone.

"There are four drawers and a locking lid. I assume the key is hidden somewhere in the house upstairs, and more, that the papers we've been looking for are contained inside one of the drawers." Addison always talked like she was being filmed when she found a clue, even if there were no cameras anywhere in evidence. She called it good practice. Andy called it a pompous affectation. And I...

I had always found it strangely endearing, like a part of her was still playing mystery make-believe in the playground behind our elementary school. Nothing we saw or heard or encountered could hurt her, because it was all this wild, wonderful, totally fictional game.

I didn't find it endearing now. Like her smirk, I found it almost offensive, one more piece of proof that she was interfering with things she didn't understand, things that had never, not even for a moment, been intended for her.

"So we go upstairs and find the key," I said.

"And open a desk that's been sealed for who-knows how long, exposing potentially fragile documents to the basement air, when we don't have the light we need to take good photographs? I don't *think* so." Addison looked up as she spoke, and her smile was enough to make her intentions plain. "Andy? Kevin? Can you come over here and give me a hand with this?"

Kevin sighed as he handed me his flashlight. "Why do we have to be the ones to carry the desk all the way back up the stairs to the kitchen? You're the one who doesn't want to open it down here."

"I never said I wanted you to carry it up the stairs," said Addison, even as she stepped back to give the boys access to the desk. "You came to that conclusion all on your own. Clearly, this is a group decision."

"Keep shoveling," advised Kevin, and moved into position on one end of the desk. Andy did the same on the other end. They exchanged a nod, and Kevin said, "On three. One, two, three."

Both of them grunted as they lifted the ancient, heavy desk out of its place against the wall. I held my breath until I was sure that it wasn't going to object to this manhandling by falling to pieces. I should have had more faith in its craftsmanship. It was sturdy, unchanging and unchangeable, not some cheap piece of temporary work from Ikea or another big box store.

"Harlowe, you're up first," said Addison. "Keep your light on the stairs. I'll bring up the rear, in case I need to help prevent a slipping incident."

It was a reasonable enough order, especially given that she was stronger than me. I couldn't shake the feeling that I was somehow being punished for drawing attention off of her when I came out of my room without my glasses.

Arguing about it down here would have been pointless, so I didn't. Instead, I nodded and turned back toward the stairs, gripping the strangely sticky banister with one hand as I began to climb.

Our descent into the basement had taken such a long time that I started counting stairs, trying to get a sense of how deeply we had traveled into the ground. It was a baffling surprise when, at stair fifteen, light appeared above me, a perfect rectangle of brightness promising a world of air and leisure and time, so much time, time that burned and flickered like a candle in the dark. Time to fritter, to waste, to spend on whatever casual pleasures seemed most appealing to me. Wine, women, and song, that was the promise of that brightness. Wine, women, and song.

It felt like a trap, although I couldn't put my finger on quite how. I blinked, and the light turned hazy around the edges, the rectangle losing its sharp edges as my eyes suddenly remembered that they were damaged, that they needed corrective lenses if they were going to work properly. I blinked again, and the sharp edges were back.

None of this made any sense. I walked faster. By stair twenty, I could see the pantry on the other side of the door. By stair thirty, I was stepping off the stairs onto the landing, level with the kitchen floor.

The smell of decay struck me full in the face, as bloated and horrific as a body left washed up on the beach when the tide rolled out. I stopped where I was, gagging.

This is what we have for them, hissed a voice I'd never heard before. *Is this what we have for you?*

The voice was sweet and septic, the voice of the void whispering through the empty spaces of my mind. My mouth worked, but no sound came out. The beam of my flashlight illuminated ancient canned goods, things that should never have been pressed and preserved, canned garlic and snails and pickled eel. No wonder the last owner had left them behind.

No: the last owner had left them behind because he was dead. No moving sale for him, no giving unwanted goodies to the local food bank for others to enjoy. Port Mercy was slipping into the sea. They might have welcomed a can of jellied eels. He'd died, and we were going to die, and I didn't want this, this smell of death and decay coating the back of my throat, this prickling fuzziness at the edges of my eyes; I didn't want this. I wanted to find my family. I wanted someplace to belong, to be healthy and happy and whole. I wanted these walls to welcome me.

I wanted the sea.

But the sea didn't want my friends. I could hear them moving behind me on the stairs, but distantly, like I had somehow managed to draw ahead of them by some vast, impossible margin. If I hadn't been standing in the doorway, I would have worried about it slamming shut and separating us.

It didn't need to separate us. We were already drifting apart, already caught in a different, tireless tide.

"No," I whispered.

Ours or theirs. One thing or the other. You are ours or you are theirs.

It sounded so reasonable, put like that: it sounded like a decision, and not an ultimatum. Addison was already done with this part of her life, already looking ahead; I had been deluding myself by pretending that one more big payday would somehow convince her to keep wasting her time on mysteries that got us five minutes of fame and a few nasty internet memes and nothing more long-lasting. She was ready to begin her adult life, ready to find a career that actually fulfilled her and a partner to share her days with. She was done. And where she went, Andy would always, inevitably follow, drawn along behind her like a balloon on a string. He cared about me, and Kevin, and our work, but his sister was the star he steered by.

Kevin...

Kevin was my brother. Kevin had saved me when we were children, even if neither of us had realized what he'd been doing at the time; we'd been too young and too lost and too desperate to figure out where we belonged to recognize salvation when we saw it. He loved me. I loved him. Nothing was ever going to change that, and for a moment—a single shining moment—it felt like that love might be enough. I could turn away from the voice that shouldn't have been whispering in my ears, I could tell the others that we had to leave, and maybe Addy and Andy would listen and maybe they wouldn't, but *Kevin* would listen, and that was what mattered. I could take my brother and run. Back to his mother's house, with the candy-colored walls and the chickens in the yard and the first bedroom that had ever felt like it was really mine. I could save him from a fate I didn't understand yet, but which loomed, formless and dreadful, over us all.

I'd need glasses again. I knew that, as sure as I knew that I would never sleep another night without hearing the whisper of the water in my veins. Wherever I went, Spindrift House would go with me, and that was only right, that was only fair: there should be a price for trespassing this far. There should always be a price. But I could run. I had the option.

Kevin swore behind me, voice low and muted, like he was trying not to be a bother. There was a jarring crunch, and then the sound of a body rolling down an uncounted number of steps. Addison screamed. Andy didn't make a sound. I whipped around, staring down into the dark, and knew that my choices, narrow as they'd already been, had just grown even narrower, even if I couldn't say exactly why.

The smell of decay faded from my nostrils. I barely noticed it go.

3.

Together, Kevin and Addison were able to wrestle the desk the rest of the way up the stairs and through the door into the pantry. They had to. Letting go of it would have turned the basement steps into a Rube-Goldberg machine of death, and finding a way to get to Andy was more important than anything else.

Getting the desk *out* of the pantry was harder. It was too large, and the room was too small, and it jutted out at an angle that made it difficult to get around. It didn't help that Addison was on the verge of losing her composure, and was snapping at both me and Kevin as we struggled to shift the heavy piece of hardwood furniture.

"Hurry *up!*" she demanded, voice gone shrill. "My brother needs help!"

"So go help him," said Kevin. "We need to get this out of the way, or we're not going to be able to get him into the kitchen once we get him up the stairs."

Addison froze, and I saw the truth in her wide, glassy eyes: she didn't want to go back down the stairs alone, because she didn't know what she was going to find at the bottom. Andy hadn't made a sound since he'd fallen. That could mean he'd hit his head on the way down. It could also mean something a lot worse. It was understandable that she didn't want to go down there alone.

That didn't change the fact that until the desk was out of the way, I couldn't *reach* the stairs, much less go down to help Andy. I wasn't as panicked as Addison. Only Kevin seemed halfway calm, although I couldn't have said whether that was due to the lingering marijuana in his system, or because he had traveled all the way through panic and into the safe harbor of some welcoming, emotionally stagnant place on the other side.

He'd been able to access that place, if only rarely, since we were kids. It was where he was at his most efficient, his most capable of handling a crisis. It was also dangerous, because when he snapped out of it, he was going to fall utterly to pieces. Right now, that was fine. I'd hand-feed him his magic brownies and pet his hair if it meant we got the desk out of the way before Addison worried her way into a heart attack.

"Harlowe, shift about half a foot to your left," he said. "Addy, put your hands here, and *push*."

I shifted. They pushed. And through the strange geometry of effort and architecture, the desk finally let go of its stubborn grasp on the doorframe and popped loose, nearly knocking me over as their formerly reasonable effort was transformed into way, way too much. I stumbled but got my feet under me, grasping the edge of the desk and crab-walking it into the center of the kitchen.

In the Shadow of Spindrift House

Addy didn't wait for us to find a safe place to put the desk down. She let go, leaving Kevin staggering before he, too, lost his grip, and the desk's legs slammed to the kitchen floor with a sickening splintering sound. There wasn't time to see whether we'd damaged the desk, the house, or both; she was already grabbing Kevin by the sleeve and dragging him with her, back into the shadows of the basement stairs.

I followed them, urgency spurring my own steps, until I was in the doorway and the stairs were leering at me, filled with shadows that seemed to twist and tangle and grab, like they were living things and not merely the absence of light. Turning my flashlight on them didn't help: instead, it created the singular impression that the shadows were actively avoiding my beam, ducking to the side and creating clear channels for their darkness to slide along.

I caught a glimpse of the back of Kevin's shirt before my beam reached its limits. I charged after him, one hand on the banister, hoping I wasn't going to trip and follow Andy to the bottom of the stairs.

The basement air was still and sweetly fungal, just like it had been before, with no trace of dampness or decay. The conviction that Andy was lying dead on the floor below us was growing, taking root in the fertile soil of my fear. I ran faster, faster, and all three of us reached the bottom at roughly the same time, and there was Andy, his face turned toward the ceiling, a halo of blood around his head, already soaking into the oiled dirt floor. His eyes were closed.

Addison moved toward him, hands outstretched. Kevin grabbed her arm. She whipped around, giving him a wounded, venomous look.

"No," he said. "Andy's breathing. See?" He pointed to Andy's chest—which was, indeed, rising and falling in a slow, almost sedated rhythm. "Give me a second to check him out, make sure he doesn't have any broken bones."

"He's my *brother*," said Addison.

"And he's my friend," said Kevin. "Let me help him."

Throat working as she swallowed, Addison nodded, and stepped aside.

Kevin knelt next to Andy. "Harley, keep the light here, all right?" he said, jabbing a finger toward the center of Andy's chest. "I can do the rest."

"Got it," I said. Aiming a flashlight was nothing. Aiming a flashlight was *easy*. What Kevin was doing...

That wasn't easy. He was doing it anyway. Even I could sometimes be surprised by the ways in which

Kevin was stronger than the rest of us, like he spent so much time in a state of low-grade panic that when the need arose, he could find serenity in the midst of situations that would have left me hiding in the nearest closet. Carefully, he ran his hands along Andy's arms and legs, slid them behind Andy's head and felt the other man's neck and skull, and finally checked to be sure his airway was unobstructed. When he straightened up again, his face was grim, but with an element of relief, like he'd found what he'd been hoping to find.

"He could still have some sort of spinal injury, and we should hold him as still as possible while we're carrying him up the stairs, but his arms and legs aren't broken, and I can't feel any obvious trauma to his head or neck," he said. "It's not going to get any safer to move him."

"Wait," said Addison. "Shouldn't we call an ambulance? Or something?"

"The nearest hospital is at least an hour away," I said, remembering what our "hosts" had told us about ordering takeout. "We can't leave him down here for an hour. It's cold."

"Harley's right," said Kevin. "Addison, you get his head. Harley, get his feet. We'll lift on three."

What followed felt oddly like a replay of moving the desk, only this time Addison and I were helping, not flanking the boys. We carried Andy through the dark, unable to aim our flashlights and hold him at the same time, and he didn't move, and he didn't make a sound.

The door's going to be closed, I thought, and this inner voice was my own, familiar and intrusive and unwanted. *You had one shot at getting out of here, and you didn't take it, and now the door's going to be closed.*

We kept climbing, until the light coming through the open pantry door chased the voice away, banishing it back into the dungeon of my doubts. We stepped into the clean light of the pantry, Andy in our arms, and Kevin nodded toward the hallway door. The living room wasn't far. Better to put Andy on something soft, like one of the sheet-draped couches, than to stretch him out on a kitchen counter, as if he were nothing but a cut of meat.

Everything is meat, whispered a voice at the back of my mind, and this time I didn't know whether it was mine or someone—something—else's. The question was enough to make my head spin. If there's any place I should be able to trust an intrusive thought to belong to me and me alone, it's in the privacy of my own mind.

But my mind didn't feel entirely like my own anymore. If I was being honest, it hadn't since the first time I saw the sea, the great, dark, slate-colored sea. I could still feel it calling to me, as constant as the tides, my heart beating in time with the waves that smashed themselves against the shore, sending tendrils lacing deeper and deeper into Port Mercy, bringing it closer, inch by inch, to its inevitable watery grave.

We stretched Andy out on a velvet couch covered in winding white, tugging his limbs as straight as we could, like we could somehow heal any broken bones with nothing more than our hands. Then we stepped back, all three of us, and looked at each other, waiting to see who would say what. Even Addison, whose brother was unconscious on a piece of someone else's antique furniture, didn't say anything; she just glanced from me to Kevin and back again, her motions sharp and uneasy, like the gestures of a wild thing that had somehow been trapped inside a human body, unable to escape, unsure of what to do.

"He's breathing," she said.

"He is," Kevin agreed.

"I don't think—" she began, and caught herself, stopping before the sentence could progress any further. My stomach sank. I knew that tone. I had heard that tone before. We all had, even Andy, who would probably have laughed, if he'd been awake.

Addison didn't like giving up. Addison didn't like admitting defeat. If we'd grabbed Andy and run straight for the car, we might have been able to get her outside before she'd realized what was happening; she might have been willing to leave. Even eager. He was her brother. He was the thing she loved best in all the world, better than she loved money, or mysteries, or being looked at as the kind of cool, competent woman who could guide her somewhat strange friends through their wild adventures.

But the moment had passed, and we weren't going to get another try at Spindrift House. If we left, even to take Andy to the hospital, we were leaving for good. Nausea warred with sudden, bitter relief, filling my mouth and throat, almost choking me. We could get out. We could run. I knew, somehow—or I hoped, anyway, and knowing and hoping were close enough to the same thing that I clung to them both with equal fervor—that if we left *now*, my vision would blur until

IN THE Shadow OF Spindrift House

I needed the familiar weight of my glasses perched on my nose for the rest of my life, however long that happened to be. My heartbeat would remember the tempo it had held for my entire life, letting go of the ceaseless stutter of the sea. My dreams would be my own again; the voices in my head, doubly so.

All we had to do was walk away.

This is the last time we can do this, I thought, and there was no one in my head but me, and it didn't matter, because I looked at the expression on Addison's face and saw the future, stretching out like a fisherman's line. The house had been the lure; the desk in the basement, hidden behind the secret door, had been the bait. We weren't going to leave here. No matter how much I wanted to, Addison was never going to allow it.

As if my thought had reminded her that she had a voice, Addison said, "Andy loves a good mystery as much as the rest of us do. More, even; he's the one who always used to say that we only needed one big success to lay the world at our feet."

"Addy," protested Kevin. There was no heat in his voice: he sounded as resigned as I felt. He knew. He'd always known.

The front door wasn't locked, but that didn't mean it was going to open for our sakes.

"No," she said. "No, it's true. He's *fine*. Andy's *fine*. He doesn't have any broken bones, he's breathing, and he has the thickest head of anyone I've ever met. He just knocked himself unconscious on the floor, that's all. When he wakes up, if we're not still in the house, he's going to be pissed. You know he is. There's no way he'd want to be the reason we missed out on a mystery as big as this one."

"You mean a payday," said Kevin. I winced, but I didn't contradict him. He'd always been braver than me, where Addy was concerned. I was too in love with her. I'd been too in love with her basically from the first time she'd looked at me with a smile on her face and a calculating plan for mayhem and mischief unfolding in her eyes. I couldn't argue with her. It would have been like fighting with the sun.

"So what if I do?" She lifted her chin and glared at him. "I'm allowed to care about myself and other people at the same time."

Before anyone could say anything else, Andy groaned. Addison was immediately at his side, crouching down so that her hair fell in a shining curtain around them, fumbling for his hand.

"Andy?" she said, breathless, eager. "Are you all right?"

Andy opened his eyes.

The room was dark; Addison's hair was darker, a spool of black thread filled with glints of light, like bioluminescent fish darting through the depths, unseen by human eyes. Andy's eyes were dark, too, like his sister's, like the sea. They always had been. But I looked at them now, and I shivered, because the intelligence that looked back at me, for all that it was vibrant, alive, and aware...

Wasn't Andy's. I stood in a room with two of my best friends, watching one of them embrace the body of the third, and wondered how I could convince them—how I could convince *myself*—that he wasn't there anymore.

Something else had come to Spindrift House. Or maybe it had been waiting for us all along.

"Harley?" Kevin's voice sounded very far away. "Harley, are you okay?"

A black pit opened in my consciousness, and I tumbled gratefully into it, away from all these impossible horrors. I heard Kevin shouting. I never felt myself hit the floor.

Chapter 6:
On the Precipice of Eternity

1.

The sea came first: the sea comes after. The middle is a long, aching desert, land rising from the depths and learning what it is to be dry, to be desiccated, to be cut off from the comforting deep. It is a punishment, a purgatory, and when it ends, as it must one day end, all the heavens will rejoice, for the sky is a sea in its own right, black and terrible and liquid. In that starry sea, what miracles may move themselves, what unspoken, unspeakable minds may drift and dream their endless dreams! It is a blessed thing, to feel the eyes of the heavens turn upon the resting blue-green sphere of the world, where the newest denizens of the cosmos yet await their turn among the stars.

I am here and I am not here and I am afraid. I can't remember my name and I can't remember what my hands are supposed to look like and I can't remember whether I'm fleeing from danger or running toward safety, but I know that I am afraid, and somehow, that knowledge is enough to soothe me. Fear is something that belongs to me, something I'm sure originates inside the coral chamber of my ribcage, deep inside the shattered shipwreck hollow of my heart. There's nothing else that's mine. Not here. Not anymore.

"We waited so long," says a voice, and it's my voice, the voice of the thoughts I didn't want to claim as my own, and it's Andy's voice, the voice of a beloved friend who swore to stay beside me through anything and everything the world could throw at us, and it's neither of those voices.

It's the voice of Spindrift House. It's old, and it's tired, and it's lonely. *So lonely that it aches, like a drowned man drawn by the weight of his own sorrows to the bottom of the sea. I feel sorry for it, and I don't want to. It doesn't deserve my sorrow, or my pity. All it deserves is my fear.*

"*Wait a little longer,*" *I say.*

"*Oh, child,*" *it sighs.* "*It's too late now. Harlowe Upton. Welcome home. We have been waiting for you.*"

I can't breathe. I can't breathe. I can't—

"Harley, come on. This isn't funny anymore. Wake up. Please?" Kevin wasn't even trying to conceal his anxiety. He normally did, at least a little; it made people uncomfortable when they realized how anxious he was, and *them* being uncomfortable was enough to make *him* even more anxious, a vicious circle that always seemed to end with him hyperventilating behind the nearest piece of cover while I punched some well-meaning asshole in the throat.

Throat-punching is surprisingly soothing, when done correctly.

I opened my eyes. I wasn't on one of those dusty old velvet couches, thank God; I was back in my own borrowed bedroom, stretched out on top of the covers, with my own pillow shoved under my head at a lumpy, somewhat unfortunate angle. The light was on. One of the bulbs had burned out, filling the room with watery shadows. I made a stilted sound of protest.

Kevin grabbed my hand in his own, squeezing tightly. "Harley, are you okay? Say something if you're okay. Say you want to get out of here, and I'll have us in a nice, safe motel by midnight."

"What about...the money," I whispered. It didn't come out as a question. I lacked the strength for the upward inflection.

"*Fuck* the money."

His voice was surprisingly vicious. I managed to turn my head enough to blink at him. He glowered back at me.

"We don't need the money," he said. "So what if we don't have insurance? We don't *need* to be professional mystery-chasers, either. Mom loves having us at home. We can take care of the house, feed the chickens, and work the stall at the farmer's market. We can pick up part-time jobs to help Mom with the bills until we find something we actually like, but between her and the farm, it's not like we're going to go hungry."

"Kevin. Do you hear what you're saying?"

"Yeah. I'm saying my sister is more important than some mythical payday that probably won't happen even if we solve this stupid mystery." He shook his head. "Andy's not right. You know it too. You maybe even know it more than I do. I saw it in your face before you fell down. Andy's not right, and it scared you bad enough that you passed out. Addy doesn't see it. She doesn't *want* to see it. She wants everything to be okay so she can stay here and keep on looking for a way to buy herself the perfect life. You know that even if we somehow did get paid, that wouldn't be enough to keep the band together, right? Addy already has one foot out the door. She's not going to stay."

"I know," I admitted.

"So why…?"

"I don't know." Slowly, I sat up on the bed, hugging my knees against my chest, the way I used to when I was a little girl and still an occasional guest in Kevin's house, not his sister yet, not his family. "I guess because it's the only thing left to try. She's my friend. She's part of the gang. The three of you saved my life when you decided you wanted me to help you find a mummy. I don't want it to be over."

"I think maybe it already is," said Kevin uncomfortably. "Something's really wrong with Andy, and Addy isn't going to leave until she has all the answers, even if they aren't good things to have. Some mysteries aren't meant to be solved. This house is haunted, remember? I don't want our ghosts to join the rest of them. I want…I want sunshine and chickens and you. I want you to yell at me until I agree to go out after it rains and help you rescue toads from the road. I want to be those weird adults on the edge of town who give cookies and lemonade and strangely specific advice to the next generation of teen sleuths. Don't you?"

"I do," I admitted. "I want to leave, Kevin, I really do. But I want to know what this house knows even more. That woman in the picture looked just like me. This is where my family's from."

"And your eyes got better, which is supposed to be impossible, and that doesn't seem to scare you nearly as much as it ought to," said Kevin grimly. "This house isn't good for you, Harley. It isn't good for *us*. I don't want to be here anymore."

"All right." I leaned over, resting my head against his shoulder, my knees still bundled to my chest, so that I was almost entirely balled up. Kevin put an arm around me, and I thought, not for the first time, how nice it was to have a brother: how good, how simple it was to have someone I trusted enough to let them see me like this. "All right. I'll make you a deal."

"I'm listening," said Kevin. There was a note of wary resignation in his voice, like he knew that he'd already lost.

"One more day," I said. "Long enough to get that desk open, and to give Andy time to snap out of whatever weird funk he's in. Then, if we're not closer to a solution, we go. We grab our stuff and we get the hell out of here. Okay?"

"Okay," he said, and kissed my forehead. His lips were cold. I closed my eyes and let him keep holding me for a little while longer. It was my choice to stay, but still. I wanted to feel safe.

Was that so much to ask?

2.

Dawn threw multicolor tendrils across the sky, pink and orange and arterial red sliding through the darkness, ripping it away. Most of the windows were shuttered, but the ones we'd opened were more than willing to let the light inside, flooding the hallways as sure as the tides flooded the town below.

Kevin had fallen asleep by my bedside, his arms still wrapped around me as he'd slumped forward and started gently snoring. That wasn't as unusual an occurrence as it would have been once, before we'd figured out that I was gay and he wasn't interested and so it was fine for us to be comfortable around each other; our shared mother wasn't going to come into one of our rooms and discover that we had decided to get frisky in the night.

It took me several minutes to disentangle myself from him and leave him sprawled across my bed, one hand still cupping my phantom shoulder. I paused to grab my glasses, out of habit, but didn't slip them on. Instead, I cupped them in my left hand, like some sort of talisman against the house and all its tricks.

Dawn pursued me down the hall to the kitchen, where the lights were bright flames of rising sunlight, and where the thing that wasn't Andy stood by the stove, eggs sizzling softly away in a cast iron pan he must have found in one of the cabinets, since I'd never seen it before. I stopped in the doorway, watching him.

I could have been wrong. He moved like Andy, flipped the eggs like Andy, had the same fluid, thoughtless grace as Andy; I could easily have dismissed all the things that struck me as wrong as being the children of an over-active mind, nightmares lingering into the glittering light of morning.

Then he turned, spatula still in his hand, and he smiled at me, and it wasn't Andy's smile, and his eyes were too bright, burning with a hectic brilliance that had no place in a human face. He blinked and the brightness was gone. The wrongness of his smile remained.

"Welcome back to the world of the living, Harlowe," he said, and his voice was Andy's and wasn't at the same time. The stresses on the words were wrong, overwriting Andy's Chicago roots with something closer to Port Mercy, something damp and drowned and buried in New England's shoals. "Did you rest well?"

"Get out of my friend," I blurted.

Not-Andy raised his stolen eyebrows in mock surprise. Then he smirked, and asked, "Would it please you to see him collapse to the floor, so much cooling meat? Would it delight your true love, his sister, to know that the other half of her heart died while she was trying to steal from a house that wasn't hers? He didn't suffer, Harlowe, if that's what you're worried about. There wasn't time for suffering. He fell, and it was over, and there was an opening, and I took it. I wanted to see you in the air, with eyes that knew the shape of you before I opened them."

I stared at him, clutching the doorframe with my free hand to keep myself from falling. "Please say this is some sort of joke, Andy," I said, and my voice was small, tight, and fragile: the voice of a child being confronted by some horror beyond imagination.

Not-Andy cocked his head. "You say I'm not him, and then you call me by his name," he said, voice mild. The eggs continued to sizzle as they fried. "You'll have to choose one side or the other eventually, Harlowe. You'll have to decide which matters more to you, the possible or the true. It's a sad state of affairs when you can't have them both, but here we are, and this is what we have to work with."

"You have no right," I whispered.

"Does a hermit crab have a right to the shell it finds on the bottom of the sea? Once the original occupant moves on, it's only gross sentimentality that connects a corpse in any way to its former owner. I didn't push your friend down those stairs, if that's what you're trying to accuse me of. Our relationship is still too fragile for that, and we don't want you to leave us before we've had the chance to know you better."

Not-Andy turned back to the stove, where the eggs hissed and spat in their pools of butter. "I took nothing that hadn't been abandoned. I had every right. Scavengers are as much a part of the natural world as predators."

Pain laced through my hand. I looked down. I was squeezing my glasses so hard that the frames were cutting into my palm, solid, modern titanium, designed to take a world of punishment without breaking.

All this had started when I'd taken off my glasses. Childhood logic said that I could make it stop by putting them back on. So I raised them to my face and slid them onto my nose, hooking their arms around my ears. The weight was a comfort; the pressure more so. Having my glasses meant being able to see where I was, to move through the world with at least a semblance of confidence.

Not this time. As soon as the lenses settled in front of my eyes, the world became a warped, terrifying tableau, as if someone had smeared the glass in a thick layer of grease and soot. Colors bled into each other, until nothing was clean, nothing was clear: it was all a mess of swirls and streaks, like fingerprints on a dirty window.

All except for Andy, who no longer looked like Andy at all, not even a little bit, not even when I stumbled backward in my shock, into the shadows of the hall. He looked like two separate, utterly distinct people at the same time, and only one of them was human.

The first man, the human man, seemed to be visible almost entirely through my left eye. He was tall and trim and nattily dressed, with long black hair and gray eyes and skin almost exactly the same color as my own, skin that would look unhealthy and lifeless too far from the coast, without the sea air to wash over and revitalize it. He was shockingly handsome, in a way that had nothing to do with sexual attraction: he was beautiful the same way a lighthouse or a sailing ship is beautiful, all aesthetic and no appeal.

The other man, though, the one I saw through my right eye...

He wasn't human. Humanity had kissed his brow once upon a time, had whispered the secrets of an upright spine and a primate's pelvis to him, had told him of the wonders of nimble fingers and strong, grasping thumbs, but that was where the resemblance ended. He wore no clothes. He didn't need them; scales covered every inch of his body, green and blue and white and gold, glittering like sunken treasure in the bloody light of dawn. His face was batrachian, wide-mouthed, flat, with the largest eyes I'd ever seen. They were the only commonality between him and the man on the left, colored gray as fog, gray as whitecaps in the moment before they struck the shore, and they were the same man, and neither of them was Andy, and neither of them was among the living.

I made a sound. I removed my glasses. The two strangers disappeared, replaced by Andy's calm, familiar face. More than ever, I couldn't shake away the knowledge that someone else was watching me through his eyes. Some*thing* else.

"So you know me now, child," he said approvingly. "Good. Very good. This will be easier if you know me."

"What are you?" I whispered.

"Your ancestor, many generations removed, for a beginning; I didn't provide the seed that grew into your mother, but I still had part of the making of you. Your blood and mine flow from the same sea."

I stared at him in silence, unable to understand.

"She shouldn't have taken you from us. She shouldn't have dared." His lips twisted downward, his eyes going hard, and if Kevin or Addison had walked into the kitchen in that moment, they would have known that something was wrong: they would have known that this man wasn't Andy. "Her grandmother was more sensible, but then, Violet married a local boy, a cousin, who understood why she needed to stay near the sea, who raised her son with at least a partial understanding of his place. Your mother was too willful. She thought that if she dropped her blood into a different ocean, the waves would overwhelm her contribution. She thought she could spare you, when all she could ever have done was steal you. She was punished, as all thieves are punished, but still, you have my apologies, Harlowe. You should have grown up here, with us. You should have *understood*."

"Understood what?" I asked. My voice broke.

He smiled, and it was neither kind nor cruel, but the expression of something inhuman trying to mimic an incomprehensible gesture. He wanted to soothe me. He succeeded in doing exactly the opposite.

"That you belong here." He stepped away from the stove, crossing the kitchen in what felt like an instant, like the flicker of an eye. Before I could even consider moving he was upon me, his hands clutching my shoulders, and they still felt like Andy's hands, like the hands that had held my hair when I drank too much, that had massaged the tension from my temples when research had resulted in eyestrain and migraines. They felt like a friend's hands, and maybe that's why I didn't pull away quickly enough. Maybe that's why he was able to pull me closer to him, smiling all the while, and his eyes were dark brown, and his eyes were gray, and I was falling into them, and I was screaming, and Andy was gone, and I was alone with this stranger who knew me better than I knew myself and this was

This was

This was my

This was my fault, and I was falling, and there was nothing but the endless sea reaching up to catch and claim me, and this was how it had always been meant to be, this was how it had always been intended to end, this was all that I deserved, this was all

This was all.

3.

The air at the top of the house was cooler than the air at the bottom, sweet with the smell of the sea. Gulls cried from the quickly brightening sky, their wings spread wide to catch the morning wind, their bellies aching for the harvest of fish that waited for them in the shallows. These weren't fat, contented parking lot gulls, happy to live their entire lives inland, well away from predator or privation: these were wild, terrible things, Mother Carey's fabled chickens, and they would peck the eyes out of the world if they thought that it would fill their stomachs.

The same creature can look very different when raised in two different environments. But their blood and bones, their scales and skin, will always remember where they were meant to be, and when they finally come home, oh. Oh, they will come home with a vengeance.

The steps didn't creak as I climbed them, and the banister was smooth under my hand, supporting me, urging me along. I tried to stop. I couldn't. My body moved entirely of its own accord, driven by the fog that had rolled off the man who had stolen Andy's body, rolled off of him and surrounded me in a shroud of soft silence.

If you need to understand, we'll show you, whispered the voice that I was half convinced belonged to Spindrift House itself. If a ghost could seize Andy and wear his body like a hermit crab wore a stolen shell, who was to say that another, larger spirit couldn't wear an entire house? Everything that's loved lives. That's what someone told me once. But when love dies, when the original thing dies, there might be other, bigger predators waiting to take what's been built and turn it to their own advantage. They might count on those deaths, like hermit crabs do, to keep them sheltered. To keep them safe.

I don't want this, I thought.

You will.

I reached the top of the stairs. The door to Addison's room was standing open, the usual welter of clothes and personal items scattered across the strip of visible floor. Of course. Of course. She was worried about her brother—she had to know that the man who was currently downstairs in our kitchen wasn't Andy. She *had* to. If I knew the Tanaka twins well, that was nothing compared to how well they knew each other. They'd been living in one another's back pockets since they were floating in their mother's womb, and when one of them was somehow compromised, the other knew it. No matter how hard Addison was trying to pretend that nothing was wrong, she knew.

I stepped into the room. She wasn't there. I tried to force my mouth to open, my lips to form her name, which was so familiar and so impossibly beloved. How many times had I whispered that name into my pillow, murmuring "Addison Upton-Tanaka" like I could somehow will her into realizing that no one was ever going to love her like I would?

If she heard me, she would understand that something was wrong, the same way she had to understand that something was wrong with Andy. She might not jump straight to "Harlowe has been possessed by the spirit of Spindrift House, and is going to do something terrible that even she doesn't fully comprehend yet." To be honest, even I was having trouble making the jump, and I was standing on the inside, as it were.

My body felt like it had been replaced by something else, some delicate construct of driftwood and seafoam, like the little mermaid in reverse. The thing that moved through me did so with surprising delicacy, until, if I closed my eyes—one of the few actions still allowed to me, as the thing didn't need to see Spindrift House to feel every beam and joint—I might as well not have existed at all. I felt my body turn away from Addison's empty room. I didn't open my eyes.

Even before I—we—reached the stairs, I knew where I was going.

The air was even cooler in the attic, even more sweetly flavored with the taste of the sea. I heard a rustle and I opened my eyes as I finished my pivot toward Addison, who was kneeling in the midst of a spiral of papers and photographs, each one laid out as precisely as the curvature of a shell.

She looked up, tucking her hair back behind one ear in a casual, almost careless motion. How I wanted to bury my fingers in that hair, even just once; even just one last time. "Harley?" she said uncertainly. "What are you doing up here? Is Andy all right?"

"I came to help." The voice was mine: the words weren't. Against my volition, my body walked over to kneel just outside the border of her spiral, leaning forward to rest my fingertips against the edge of what I now knew was a photo of Violet Upton. She was older in this picture than she was in the last one, her hair longer, the hollows around her eyes more pronounced; she balanced a baby on her hip, the child dressed in a winding white gown that said nothing about whether it was a boy or girl, not given the time period. "Do you know who this is yet?"

"No." Addison shook her head, hair coming free and falling into her face once more. "I think she's one of the original owners, or maybe the wife of one of the original owners, but it's hard to tell when they didn't bother to properly label much of anything."

"Do you think the labels might be in the desk?"

For the first time, I could see the fear flicker in her eyes. "I don't want to open it until Andy says it's all right. He's the one who fell. He should get to decide."

"Have you asked him?"

Addison turned her face away.

Please don't do this, I thought, as loudly and as fiercely as I could. *Please let her go.*

Too late, purred the voice of the house. *She doesn't belong here.*

Neither do I.

Oh, my dearest girl, that's where you're wrong. That's where you're so very, very wrong.

"Are you afraid of Andy, Addison?" The thing that was controlling my voice managed to make the question gentle, almost kind, like it was coming from a place of genuine concern, and not from one of infinite, ageless malice.

"I don't know." She looked back defiantly. "He's my brother. I love him. I'm afraid *for* him. He should be in

a hospital right now, not wandering around this haz-
ardous old pile of a house. I hope that once we find out
who owns it, that person drops a match in the middle
of the living room and watches it all burn. The value
here's in the land, anyway."

"If you're so worried about him, why not leave?"
The question could have been my own. I stared at her
from behind my own eyes, willing her to see me, to
understand how much danger she was in, to *run*. Andy
was already dead. She'd be leaving nothing but a corpse
behind. But she could take Kevin, if she was quick
about it. She could save my brother, if not her own.

She couldn't save me. Saving me was out of the
question. The house was moving in my veins, burrow-
ing into my bones, and while I wanted it out of my
mind, I was finding it harder and harder to think of its
occupation as a violation. I had entered it first, after all.
It was only fair that it should, when given the opportunity, decide to enter me in turn. I was lost, and she was
rapidly approaching the point at which she'd join me,
if she didn't see the danger she was in before it was too
late. If she didn't run.

"The money." Her laugh was thin and bitter.
"God, Harlowe, you dangle that much money in

front of me and then you ask me why I don't leave? Why not go out there and ask the ocean why it's so damn wet? I want the money, and I know we can solve this fucking mystery. Andy has a concussion or something. Whatever. He's got a thick head, and he's still standing, and once we have that check, we'll be able to pay for all the medical care in the world. He took worse hits when he was playing football back in high school. He'll be fine. And I know Kevin has some stupid idea about playing gentleman farmer and living off his inheritance or whatever, and you'll probably go along with him because it's easier, but not me. Not Addison Tanaka. I'm going to make something of myself, and you can't make anything without the raw materials."

"I see." I did, really, and so did the thing that had seized my body; for that moment, we were united.

I had done this to her. I had dangled a mystery and a monumental amount of money in front of her face, and I'd done it because I hadn't wanted her to leave me, but it had been the necessary lure to get her here, to Spindrift House, to one more adventure, to one more chance for her to realize that she needed me as much as I needed her. Only I hadn't succeeded, had I? She was looking at me the way she always had…and for the first time, I supposed that was a mercy. She'd been dead from the moment we stepped through the front door. If she'd been dead and finally able to love me back, it might have broken me.

The fact that her death wasn't breaking me anyway should probably have been terrifying. But it wasn't. My body stood, taking me with it, and offered Addison one familiar hand. The nails were bitten to the quick, as always; the fingers were calloused. It was mine, and it might as well have belonged to a stranger.

"I saw something yesterday, when we were out on the widow's walk," said my voice. "Come on. I'll show you. Maybe it can answer some of your questions."

"How come you're the one who keeps finding all the clues?" she asked, suddenly suspicious.

Too late, Addison, too late, too late; you should have started to suspect as soon as I found the door in the pantry, as soon as you saw that stairway down into the dark. But she hadn't, and now here we were, my body but not my mind holding out a hand for her to take, and her slowly, inevitably taking it, allowing herself to be led to the open door onto the outside world, where the widow's walk was waiting.

The wind whispered sweet lies around us, the same sweet lies it had told so many others, and the sky was bloody with the dawn, red and orange and yellow blending into blue, like the sea washing away the signs of a brutal, unforgiveable murder. Step by step, the thing that was not me used my body to lead Addison around the side of the house, and if she went willingly, maybe that was the house as well; maybe that was the air, filled with the bitterness of a decay I had only briefly tasted, because I, unlike my friends, was wanted here.

Together, the three of us walked along the narrow wooden path that hugged the peak of the house, protected from the fall by only a low, filigreed wall. It was delicate. There was no wood rot in Spindrift House, no sign that the elements had ever been gauche enough to have their way with this ageless, unkind edifice, but the wood of the wall was thin, easily broken, easily repaired.

We stopped when we reached the corner overlooking the sea. Addison turned to look at me—at us—but there was no eagerness in her eyes, only a low, muted expectation.

"You're not Harlowe, are you?" she asked.

My eyebrow rose; my lips moved. "What makes you say that?" my voice asked.

Her laughter was a mourner's moan. "Harlowe is one of my best friends. I love her dearly, even if she's a research-obsessed weirdo. But I don't love her the same way she loves me, and when I look at you, I don't see any of that love. It isn't there."

"Maybe I'm just mad at you."

Addison shook her head. The dawnlight struck bloody glints off her hair. "You don't fall out of love that fast, if you fall out of love at all. No. If you were Harlowe, you'd love me, and you don't love me, and that means you're not Harlowe. Answer me one question, please."

"What's that?" asked the spirit of Spindrift House, amusement in its tone.

"Is my brother dead?"

Smiling, the spirit nodded with my head. Addison nodded back.

"I thought so," she said, and struck.

She had always been fast. She had always been brutal. Now, fighting for her life against the ghost that had seized the body of her best friend, she was relentless. She moved like water over stones, and I was so proud of her it ached, even as her knuckles slammed into the skin of my throat like a freight train.

It didn't hurt. My pride faded, replaced by fear. Spindrift House felt no pain. Why should it? To be a house was to be above such petty human concerns. It stood tall and proud and let her come, let her assault its stolen human form, let her exhaust herself against it as a wave is exhausted against the shore. And when she began to tire, when she began to slow, when realization blossomed in her eyes, it reached out with my hand and seized her by the throat before she could turn to run away.

"My turn," it said, and lifted her up and flung her over the side, into the empty air.

She screamed the whole way down. She screamed and kicked and clawed at the sky, hands hooked like she thought if she could just find something to drive them into, she could anchor herself, stopping her descent and leaving her forever suspended in the moment before her death.

I wanted to turn away. I wanted to close my eyes. Spindrift House wouldn't allow me to do either of those things. They would have seemed too much like kindness, too much like mercy; they would have allowed me the illusion that she hadn't suffered when she finally hit the ground.

Addison slammed into the cliffside like a stone dropped into the sea. There was a terrible crashing sound as pieces of her smashed. Worst of all, she didn't die on impact. She had time to twitch, slow and dreadful, and to fix her eyes on me. I was too far away. I shouldn't have been able to see the accusation there. I saw it clear as day.

She coughed once, twice, and a bubble of blood formed between her lips, popping and running down her cheek before she was finally still, and I was finally allowed to close my eyes.

Now, purred the voice of Spindrift House. *We begin.*

Part III:
Flood Tide

Chapter 7:
Before the Last Ship Sails

1.

Once again, I opened my eyes to find myself looking at the ceiling of my borrowed bedroom. Kevin was still sitting next to the bed, bent forward so that his forehead rested on his arms, snoring gently. I blinked at him blearily, wiping my eyes before reaching. Then I sat up, sudden excitement flooding through me.

Maybe it had all been a dream. Like the dreams about Violet Upton, or about the house itself. Maybe no one had ever seized my body, or used me as a murder weapon. Maybe Andy was still himself, and Addison was…Addison was…

Maybe Addison was fine.

Kevin made a soft grumbling noise, shifting position slightly as he went back to snoring. I smiled at him fondly. My brother. I'd never expected to have one, being an orphan and everything, and it was all too easy to imagine what my life would have been like without him, without the rest of the Answer Squad. They had saved me in every possible way.

My smile faded. They had saved me, and I had rewarded them by leading them here, off the edges of the known world, into a place where nothing good could thrive for long. The angles of the walls were abhorrent, too straight, too clean. How could anything live in a place where everything stood in such defiance of natural, normal geometry? It was vile. Unspeakable.

Home.

Not Spindrift House itself, but the thing it represented, the great, teeming thing on the other side of the ceaseless heartbeat of the waiting sea. As if the thought had been enough to break some inner barrier, my head began to pound, in time with those battering waves. I ground the heels of my hands into my temples, trying to stop the sound. It didn't help. It washed over me again and again, and I knew, absolutely and without question, that while I might have been dreaming before—might have imagined every step between my bedroom and Addison's descent—it would all come true if I didn't get us out of here as soon as possible.

I dropped my hands and reached, automatically, for the glasses on my nightstand. They weren't there. My hand closed on nothing, and I knew that they weren't under the bed, knocked out of place by a clumsy dreamland gesture, and they weren't on the dresser; they were gone. They'd been lost somewhere between the kitchen and the widow's walk. If I concentrated, I could almost remember seeing them tumble into the void after Addison, thrown away by a careless hand. *My* hand, even if I hadn't been the one behind it.

My moans were low and bestial, filling the room with a wall of agonized sound. I wanted to wake Kevin. I wanted someone with me as I went out into the house, someone who would listen, someone who would *understand*.

But he wouldn't understand, would he? He still looked at the straight lines of the walls and saw clean, stable construction, the sort of thing that was intended to last for generations. He saw safety, comfort, home, and all I could see was an offense to nature. It was like my eyes no longer wanted to focus the way they always had, like they were seeing the world beneath the world now, and couldn't be convinced to return to their former focus.

I swallowed the last of my moans, feeling it buck and thrash like a fish in my throat, sharp-spined and desperate to escape. I nearly choked on it, and when I breathed, I could feel it, snagged there, bound tight. I slid out of the bed, pausing to kiss Kevin's temple, feeling only the sick conviction that this was the last time we were going to see each other alive.

"I'll get you back to your chickens, I promise," I whispered, and he slept on. My anxious, jumpy brother, who had always been so attuned to my moods that he sometimes woke up before I even realized I was having a nightmare, slept on.

My stomach churned. I pressed the first two fingers of my left hand against his neck, and was rewarded with the feeling of his pulse, strong and steady and undeniable. A feeling of absolute ridiculousness washed over me a moment later. Of course his heart was beating: he was breathing. Corpses don't snore. But that didn't mean the house hadn't *done* something to him, that he wasn't somehow enraptured and ensnared by its witchcraft.

"I love you," I said, and left the room.

The halls of Spindrift House were bright and airy, filled with the rays of the midday sun. Half the day had slipped away while I…slept? Hibernated? I didn't know the term for what I'd done, and without the words to frame the concept, it remained vague, half-sketched, like something out of a dream. Had I dreamt? I thought I might have. I thought I might have dreamt a deep and sunken city, a place where no straight lines, no hard angles, would ever dare to trespass. I thought I might have known myself there, known myself in a way that had never been true before and would never be true again, at least not in the harsh gravity of the sunlit world above.

I thought I might have been happy there, in the city of my dreams, drowned and drowning, deep beneath the thunder and turmoil of the waves.

The kitchen was empty this time: the breakfast dishes had long since been cleaned away. The cast iron pan hung, scrubbed clean, from its hook above the stove. The desk remained, sitting squarely in the middle of the floor like an invitation to approach.

So I approached.

Each drawer had a carved scrimshaw knob shaped like some tangled, beautiful sea creature. I didn't recognize any of them, but the largest knob, set on the rolltop of the desk itself, caught and held my eye. It was a man and a fish and a Scylla-esque swirl of tentacles all at the same time, changing when I looked at it from one angle or another. The lines of the scrimshaw itself never shifted; I could focus on one and see that it remained absolutely the same, even as the image seemed to twist and warp around it. It was an optical illusion carved from aged whalebone, and it would have been more than mystery enough in any other time, in any other place.

Here, though, there were questions to be answered—like why, when this house so clearly knew me, so clearly called to the Upton blood flowing in my veins, there could be any question as to its provenance. I approached the desk warily, as I might approach some wild, dangerous beast. When the wood failed to suddenly acquire the ability to attack, I reached out and rested my fingertips against the rolltop, bare inches away from the scrimshaw knob.

"You know me," I said softly. I barely recognized my own voice. It sounded more alien to me, now, than it had when the house had been using it on my behalf. Time was running out. Time for what, I wasn't entirely sure, but time all the same.

The desk seemed to shift and shudder under my hand. I held my ground, calling on all the courage that I had gathered to myself during my days with the Answer Squad. I could do this. I *would* do this. Andy was lost. Addison was lost. I was lost, too, had been lost maybe since the beginning, since the day years ago when I had been flipping idly through the mystery site collection of "white whales"—the cases too big and too strange and too complicated for anyone to ever have a prayer of solving them—and the fishhook image of Spindrift House had caught and kept my eye, snaring me. The house had been reeling me in since that day, and like a fish that didn't realize it was being dragged out of the depths, I had been powerless to resist.

All of us were lost, except for Kevin. And for Kevin, I would dive even deeper, would sink the hook further into my flesh, if only it would buy him the time to get away.

"You know me, and you want me, and I'm willing to listen to what you have to say, but only for a little while," I said. "If you want me to understand, this is when you tell your story. This is when you *convince* me. So come on. Convince me."

I took my hand away. There was the softest, slightest of clicks, and the knob that was man and monster and both and neither twisted, so subtly that I would have thought my eyes were lying to me, had the rolltop not begun to roll upward a moment later. I took a step back, wary of what the movement might reveal.

The desk's main writing surface was perfectly laid out, like some past scholar had been writing down their thoughts only moments before and had simply stepped away for a moment to take care of something. A black-bound ledger lay at the very center, flanked by blotting paper, inkwell, and fountain pen. I reached for the ledger. It was slick against my fingers, made of some leather that felt simultaneously repulsive and enticing. I had never felt anything so soft. I had never touched anything so slimy. Those two contradictory states weren't contradictions at all, but two sides of the same perfect coin, like this house was, like I was.

"Thank you," I said to the desk, and retreated to the table where I had sat with my friends to eat breakfast a lifetime ago, and opened the ledger, and began to read.

2.

Port Mercy, Maine. October 2, 1853.

It is good weather and better fishing on this day, and I am told that I am to be a wife. I will marry my cousin Lyall when he returns from the sea, and I am grateful for his attention. He will be a good husband, I think, and he will not question things which should not be questioned, nor will he refuse things which should not be refused.

I will be a good wife to him. I will bear him strong children, and if he is Called before my time, I will tend to his affairs here on the shore until the time is come for me to join him. I can only trust that he will do the same for me, should I be so endlessly blessed in the eyes of our Lord.

It is not mine to set the hour, only mine to count the minutes until that hour is come, and I may live eternal in the paradise which has been made for us. Time is the one treasure we have been granted in unquestioned plenty, and so I shall not question it, for to do so would be to show a lack of faith. I will not be faithless. Not like Josephine Latour, may she long repent what she has done, to run off so, and with a man from the desert! She will be fortunate indeed if ever she is welcomed home.

Spindrift House is to be mine for the keeping for this next cycle of the tides. I will prepare it for my husband, and when he arrives, we shall become one in the oldest and most glorious of rituals. Oh, I only hope that he will find me fair, for it would be terrible indeed to be netted by a man who did not love me.

Port Mercy, Maine. November 10, 1853.

My skin is alight with the memory of his hands! So soft, so rough, like the wood of a ship's hull, which can be kind and cruel in the same motion. He held me like I was his rock against an endless storm, and I am not ashamed to say that I clung to him in turn, and that together we enacted the rite which was demanded of us. There will be more Uptons in the world for our efforts, make no mistake, and if there are not, it shall not be for lack of wanting!

My father came to the wedding. I did not think to see him there, and he kept to the shadows of the church hall, that he might not frighten the clergy who would not understand the length of his limbs or the sharpness of his teeth. It is a pity, that we must live so in shadow, trembling at the thought of judgment, but so it must be until the tide changes again. We live in a time of superstition, and it would not be wise to attract too much attention. So we wed in the church, in gowns of white and suits of linen, and we pretend their bread is flesh and their wine is blood, and we wait. How we wait.

I would gladly wait all the rest of my days for my Lyall's hands against my skin, for his mouth against my throat. He is the salt to my sea, and I am the waves to his shore, and together we will build a brighter future for us and all who share our family name. We are the hook and the harbor, and as long as there are Uptons in Port Mercy, we will be sacred to the sea.

The next twenty entries were more of the same: she loved her husband, she loved her house, she loved her home town. She even loved the experience of being pregnant, of moving through the streets of Port Mercy like a ship under full sail, gravid with passengers, straining under the weight of her cargo. I skipped ahead, looking for something—anything—that might be relevant to the mystery of the house itself. Based on what I'd read so far, there shouldn't have been any question as to its ownership. Violet Upton and her husband lived there without challenge or question, and the only mention of either the Pickwells or the Latours had been the unfortunate Josephine, who had run off with a man from the desert.

My eyes settled on an entry dated nine months after the wedding.

Port Mercy, Maine. September 2, 1854.

I am delivered of a son, fine and hale and living well. His cries are lusty with rage at the world. He will grow to be as strong as we can make him. He will fill his belly with milk and bread and fish, and he will know what it is to serve the sea, and to hear the echoing voice of our Lord calling him forever home. How glorious it is to look upon his dear, distorted face, like a mashed-together mirror of mine and my Lyall's. How miraculous it is to know that one day, he will shed this clumsy, soft-skinned mien and become the handsome scion of our family line that I know his blood already longs to be.

But he is not my firstborn, and I am afraid.

My labor came hard, as the first September storm assaulted the shore. I rejoiced, for to bear a child into a gale is to bear a child who will have no illusions about the nature of the world, or what it will demand of us. A storm-born child goes from the water of the womb to the water of the open sky and is twice-blessed in the process, for they need never know dry land. Had my son, my darling boy, been the first to tear himself from my body, I would have no need for concern.

A full day and night I spent in childbed, my sisters by my side, my husband waiting in the parlor, as is only right and proper. The storm howled, and I howled with it, until midnight struck to mark the second day, and my daughter finally ripped free of the harbor that had been my body, sailing for the shore. Alas that she, like so many ships before her, crashed upon the rocks; when she slid onto the bed, she was silent and still, and did not breathe nor stir.

We have named her Rosemary. She is to be buried behind Spindrift House, where she belongs. But still, I am afraid.

Mira Grant

Port Mercy, Maine. September 10, 1854.

My fears are justified. Josiah Pickwell has come to accuse us of breaking our peace with him and his family, for was not my firstborn daughter promised to his first-born son as means of mending past wrongs? No number of testimonies as to my dear Rosemary's condition upon her arrival have made any difference to his calculating heart. To listen to the man, we should have saved her body for his son's pleasures, vile though that very thought must be to any right-thinking individual. Imagine, being so desper-ate to claim that which is not yours that you would treat a sweet, stillborn girl as a pawn to fit your hand!

Lyall has gone to the courts to appeal Josiah's demands, but I fear it will come to nothing, for the contract between our families is clear. I would not have willingly given the man a daughter under any circumstances, much less the ones which our Lord has seen fit to grant us. Still, the contract was binding, and we yet may be undone.

Port Mercy, Maine. October 1, 1854.

We are lost. Rosemary Upton is to be married, despite her age and condition, to Elijah Pickwell, and with that marriage, Spindrift House and all its lands will pass to the Pickwell family for the span of a generation. As Elijah and Rosemary can have no legal issue, given that she is but an infant, and dead beside, the house will be returned to the Upton line upon Elijah's death. The contract which would have married the first Latour daughter to his first son will be null and void, and my home will be my son's to claim.

Not mine. I do not intend to be here when that happy day arrives. I will have gone home, to live forever in the splendor and glory of my Lord.

May this village and all its people be drowned for what they've done to me, and for the dishonor they have offered my poor daughter. You deserved so much better than this, my Rosemary.

I would have given you the world. Now all I can give you are my tears.

I am so sorry, little girl. I am so deeply, truly sorry.

There was more, tangled in other entries; details of promises made and broken, of bargains that pre-dated Violet and her husband. They filled in the rest of the pieces I needed, but there weren't many, not by that point. I already knew most of it. Carefully, I set the diary aside and rose, walking to the back door. It wasn't locked. I opened it, looking out on the graveyard, the tangled weeds, the obscured headstones. There was something peaceful about it, something kind. This was where people went when their stories ended. This was where they got to rest.

"All right," I said. "I know the answer now.

"Come face me, you fuckers."

And then I closed the door, and walked back to the table, and sat down to wait.

3.

When the door opened, I didn't turn. I was too afraid that Spindrift House would have decided it knew what I wanted, and tried to give it to me. More—and more importantly—I was too afraid it would be right, because I wasn't sure what I wanted anymore.

I wanted to go home. I wanted to stand on the shore of Lake Michigan, captive, toothless sea that it was, at least in comparison to the peerless power of the unbounded Atlantic, and hold my brother's hand, and never spare another thought for the sea inside of me. I was the spindrift scion of a poisoned ocean; the blood in my veins was tainted by a hundred generations of Uptons, by a thousand rituals and small sacrifices that I could neither name nor fully understand, but could feel plucking at the edges of my consciousness, asking me to put paid to debts that were incurred before I could even be conceived. I wanted Chicago, towering spires and low, comfortable homes and straight, secure angles, lines measured and sketched and perfected long before a single cut was made. If nature abhorred a straight line, I would go where nature wasn't, and I would be happy there, I would.

But I wouldn't. Because as much as I wanted to go home, I wanted to stay here, in Port Mercy, in Spindrift House, even more. It had slipped its roots into me, maybe even before I'd seen its picture on that website: maybe when I was a toddler, when the men with knives came out of the fog and cut my parents down, leaving me an anchorless orphan. The thought of shutting myself into a world of lines and angles made my flesh crawl, pulling itself tight around my thankfully smooth, thankfully rounded bones. I carried no straight lines within my body. I was as nature wanted me to be.

But I carried the seeds of metamorphosis. I could feel them stirring, shifting, changing from one moment to the other, like the knob on the desk, the scrimshaw whalebone knob that was man and monster and both and neither. I thought he must have a name.

I thought I might learn it soon.

"What do you know?" asked a voice, and it was Addison's, and not Addison's, all at the same time. It was too soft to be hers, too free of self-concern. It was her voice as Spindrift House believed I wanted it to be, and I closed my eyes, because otherwise, I might give in to the temptation to look, to see, to *know*.

If I knew, I thought I might never be able to let her go. It was painful, all this thinking. I would be gladder than I could say when it wasn't necessary anymore.

"No," I said, calm and clear and absolutely firm. "I won't talk to you in her body. She's dead. Put her back where you found her, and come to me in Andy's skin, not hers. I'll tell you what I know when you come to me the way I tell you to."

"If I said you only got one request from me, is that what you would ask for?" Not-Addison sounded amused. "Would that be enough for you?"

"You know it wouldn't be," I said. "But I know you're not going to fight me on this. You wouldn't have tried so hard to call me back if you were going to fight me."

"Stay where you are, Harlowe Upton, and be prepared to answer my questions. My patience is not infinite, even with a child such as yourself."

The door opened and closed again and oh, I *was* a child, at least in the eyes of the ageless, terrible heart of Spindrift House, which did not beat, but chilled, compacting ever smaller, until one day it would become an egg of diamond, and when it hatched, what terrible things would come tumbling forth, ready to consume the world.

I don't think like that, I thought, and *I do now,* I thought, and here, in the poisoned perfumed air of Spindrift House, I was perfectly correct.

I sat with a child's primness, my shoulders squared, my hands folded in my lap, until I heard the door open and close again. Then I turned my face toward it, opening my eyes, and looked at the face that had belonged to Andy Tanaka, once, until a force too old and too alien for understanding had come and taken it away from him.

"Did you push him?" I asked.

It shook Andy's head. "He fell," it said. "It was convenient for us, we won't deny that, but we had no hand in his death. People grow clumsy here, when their

189

blood is not like our own. Something in the air is bad for them. If it hadn't been him, it would have been one of the others."

I nodded to show that I believed what it was saying—and I did believe it, truly. It had nothing left to gain by lying to me. "Where did you put Addison?"

"The girl?" It scoffed. "We thought you might have enjoyed speaking to her. Your heart sang when it saw her face. We don't understand the appeal. Humans all look the same to us, pale and wasted and larval. Still, we suppose it's natural for young things to love things that resemble their own kind."

"Neoteny," I said numbly. The thing I had seen when I looked at Andy's stolen body through my no-longer-necessary glasses had been aquatic, but it had been more amphibious than fish-like, hadn't it?

Who was to say what the larval form of an amphibian that walked on two legs, that was strong enough to survive the sea, might look like? Or how long those larval stages might last, how long they might *live?* I knew Violet had looked like me when she lived here, in Spindrift House, but her father...

Oh, her father. Who had attended her wedding in the very back of the church. Who hadn't let the preacher see his face. How things change. How things stay the same.

The house smiled at me with Andy's lips, nodded to me with Andy's chin. "Exactly," it said. "Now tell me: what do you know? Who owns these grounds?"

"Why does it matter?"

"There was a promise, once. There was a compact. Now, the town is nearly drowned, and the humans who once sheltered my descendants drown with it, or leave for drier places. Spindrift House will stand—it was built to stand—but it will need a caretaker, and we need to know from whose blood that caretaker will be drawn." It crooked one of Andy's eyebrows upward. "Your mother left us, carrying you away. We were able to send hands to punish her for what she had done, but there was no one here to care for you, no one left to see to your simple, fragile needs. It suited us to let you be lost for a time, and look how you've rewarded us! You know how to answer questions. Answer this one. Who do we belong to?"

I took a deep breath. "The man upstairs. Why won't he wake up?"

It shrugged. "The air," it said, as if the answer didn't matter. "He's drowning. Poetic, isn't it? Humans are such breakable creatures. He doesn't suffer, if that's your concern."

"He leaves," I said. "Alive. He leaves, and you don't send 'hands' or whatever else you want to call cultists with knives after him. He gets to walk away, and I give you all the answers you want."

The house smiled again, and the expression looked less like Andy's all the time. "Why would we do that for you?"

"Because this will be easier if I stay here willingly." Because I could feel the structures shifting beneath my skin, bits of bone breaking themselves free of my ribs and spine and positioning themselves just so, ready to grow long and sharp and venomous. Because I wasn't sure whether I could leave anymore. I thought that point might have passed already, unremarked in the face of mystery and murder and slow, grinding transformation.

"And?" There was a lilting, mocking note in Andy's voice. "What makes you think you have a choice?"

"I don't think you can steal my skin forever, or you wouldn't have left it," I said. "I think you need an Upton—and it's telling that there weren't any when we arrived in town. I think I might be the last one you have, at least for now. And if you don't let my brother go, then every time you return my mind to me, I will run for the widow's walk. You showed me how easy it is to fall from there, remember? You taught me the way to fall. Let Kevin go and I stay. Keep him here, let him drown, and find out how quickly I can die to thwart you. The choice is yours."

The smile faded from Andy's stolen lips, and I was glad to see it go. The house didn't deserve it. "You wouldn't."

"I would." I jutted my chin out stubbornly. "If Kevin were awake, you could ask him how hard it is to make me do something that I don't want to do. Do we have a deal?"

Not-Andy glared at me. "If you know what we need to know, yes. We have a deal. Now tell me, whose house is this?"

"You never said it, but you implied it: I am the last available Upton. The house should have gone to the husband of Josephine Latour."

"Hiram Upton was to marry her," said the house tersely.

"Yeah, well, he didn't, and so she surrendered her family's claim over you by breaking the betrothal. The house passed from Lyall and Violet Upton to Elijah

Pickwell when he married Rosemary Upton, but they didn't have any children, which meant the house passed *back* to the Uptons until one of them could find a suitable Latour to wed. Violet's son, Stanhope, married a cousin, Piety, and they had one daughter. Angelina Upton. My mother. She ran away to pretend to be human, and gave birth to me when she was over a hundred years old; she had no other children. This house belongs to me. Your mystery is solved." I smiled, tight and thin and furious. "Now give my brother the money and let him go."

And the house, wrapped in the rotting corpse of my friend, smiled back.

Chapter 8:
And I Alone Am Left To Tell Thee

1.

Kevin left with three and a half million dollars in his pocket and a dazed expression on his face that the house swore would fade as he put more distance between himself and the shore. He didn't seem to recognize me. That was probably for the best. He would never see me again, wouldn't even remember the names "Port Mercy" or "Spindrift House." He wouldn't be able to lead the authorities back here, to the tiny family graveyard where Andy and Addison Tanaka were going to sleep, more peacefully than the bones of my own ancestors, which did not, for the most part, rest beneath the stones that bore their names.

I stood on the porch and watched him drive away until there was nothing left for me to see, and then I turned around and went back inside.

Without a vessel, the house was reduced once more to whispers in the corners, darting shadows and strange silences. I ignored them all as I walked back to the kitchen, where I was writing out the growing list of things I was going to need if I was going to live here. And I was, at least for a while. At least until the change came for me.

2.

The sea sang in the night, and my heart sang with it, and oh, I am damned, and oh, I am finally home. When the morning broke, I opened my eyes and stared at the ceiling of the room that was no longer borrowed, the name of my Lord on my lips like a promise, like a prayer.

"Dagon," I whispered, and everything made sense at last.

3.

I'm going to need good internet. Getting it installed may be hard, but that's what the Pickwells and the Latours are for. They've just been waiting for an Upton to come home and claim their legacy again. I need a fast connection and a good computer and time.

There are cousins out there somewhere, dry and dull-eyed and unaware of the void within them, the place where the sea should be.

I'll find them. Before the tide runs out, I'll find them, and I'll bring every single one of them home. I was right about one thing, after all.

Mystery is what I do.